"Cheer up."

He leaned down toward her, getting a faint hint of perfume. Nothing heady. Nothing overdone. Just... interesting. "The year's almost done!"

"...four! Three!"

"Hallelujah for small mercies." She tilted her head toward him, leaning closer to be heard, as well.

"...two! One! Happy New Year!"

The bar went wild.

Confetti shot from every corner, showering everyone in tiny bits of colored tissue while the strains of "Auld Lang Syne" blasted from the sound system.

Mac eyed the brunette.

She had bits of blue and green clinging to her hair. A pink piece of confetti on her nose. All around them people were either kissing each other or singing.

Her eyes met his and something inside him shrugged.

He'd never been a singer.

"Happy New Year," he said, and leaned down to brush his mouth lightly against hers.

Not quite as briefly as he'd intended.

Dear Reader,

Masks. We all wear them, and no, I'm not talking about pandemic masks or Halloween masks. I'm talking about the masks we wear to hide our insecurities. Our doubts and fears.

On the outside, Delia Templeton is vibrant and beautiful. She's basically an heiress and the world should be her oyster. She's also surrounded by family members who always succeed. Who have fulfilling relationships and impressive careers and never seem to falter while she has no career; no romantic prospects. She doesn't expect anything remarkable from herself so why should anyone else? For Delia, her weighty mask makes for a cozy, warm place.

Then her very canny granny tosses her into the deep end to sink or swim. She's floundering the most when she encounters a seemingly ordinary man named Mac Jeffries who turns out to be anything *but* ordinary. Will Delia realize that when something— and someone—is important enough to fight for, masks dissolve and amazing things happen?

Remarkable things?

Like love?

Whether this is your first visit to Weaver, Wyoming, or you're a returning guest, thank you for joining me and for diving in with Delia and Mac!

Allison

Her Wyoming Valentine Wish

—

ALLISON LEIGH

HARLEQUIN
SPECIAL
EDITION

Recycling programs
for this product may
not exist in your area.

ISBN-13: 978-1-335-40834-1

Her Wyoming Valentine Wish

Copyright © 2022 by Allison Lee Johnson

This edition published by arrangement with Harlequin Books S.A.

For questions and comments about the quality of this book, please contact us at CustomerService@Harlequin.com.

Harlequin Enterprises ULC
22 Adelaide St. West, 41st Floor
Toronto, Ontario M5H 4E3, Canada
www.Harlequin.com

Printed in U.S.A.

Though her name is frequently on bestseller lists, **Allison Leigh**'s high point as a writer is hearing from readers that they laughed, cried or lost sleep while reading her books. She credits her family with great patience for the time she's parked at her computer, and for blessing her with the kind of love she wants her readers to share with the characters living in the pages of her books. Contact her at allisonleigh.com.

Visit the Author Profile page
at Harlequin.com for more titles.

Chapter One

It was her laugh that got his attention.

Full and uninhibited, it cut above all the other noise. The music. The voices.

Mac Jeffries let the door to Colbys Bar & Grill shut behind him, cutting off the cold wind outside, and automatically glanced toward the source of the laughter as he worked his way through the crowd.

He didn't see her at first. She wasn't very tall. The people around her were. But she laughed again, and someone sat down and there she was.

Young.

A looker for sure.

Her head was tilted back in laughter, her parted lips red and shining. Dark glossy hair waved around her shoulders. The sweater she wore hugged curves that would have garnered attention even if it hadn't been ruby red and sparkling.

It *was* New Year's Eve. But all that sparkle wasn't exactly the norm in these parts where dressing up meant ironing a crease into your blue jeans and wearing the cowboy hat that sported the fewest sweat stains.

He realized he was smiling a little.

He hitched his tool bag higher as he sidled between two tables and finally reached the end of the glossy wood bar. Three bartenders worked behind it, busily mixing drinks, opening wine bottles, pouring beer. Mostly pouring beer.

He lifted the hatch and joined them. "Hey, Charmaine," he greeted the bartender closest to him when she gave him a glance.

"We were about to give up on you." She simultaneously pulled tabs on two beer cans. "It's nearly midnight."

"Got here as quick as I could." He crouched down in front of the appliances lined up beneath the bar top. By trade, he was an auto mechanic. Not an appliance repairman. But he'd done his fair share of coaxing life back into all manner of things. An ice maker was one of the simpler things. "Been a busy night."

"Tell me about it." Charmaine brushed against his shoulder as she leaned past him to set a full pitcher on a tray already holding two others. The tray was immediately whisked away by a server. "We haven't had a chance to draw breath here, either."

She angled away from him as he dismantled the unit to reach the inside mechanics.

He was only there as a favor to Casey Clay, whose wife owned Colbys. If not for that, Mac would have been happy to head home to bed on the bitingly cold night.

Yeah, he'd have been alone, but what else was new?

Fortunately, this ice unit was a secondary one. Though Mac figured that a lack of ice cubes wouldn't inhibit the crowd too much that night.

Even muffled slightly by the bar he was trying to crawl beneath, he could hear another burst of the brunette's full-throttle laughter.

He wondered what *she* would be doing once the clock struck twelve but immediately brushed the thought aside and focused harder on the repair.

It was dark beneath the bar top, but he just tucked his narrow flashlight between his teeth once he'd identified the problem and set to work. All told, it took about twenty minutes to change out a section of wiring and piece the thing back together. With the ice maker humming once again, he quickly unwound from his confined position, stretching out his back with a little relief as he straightened.

She was standing on the other side of the bar. Lips still glossy. Ruby-red sweater still clinging to her curves.

Up close, her long-lashed eyes were hazel. Strikingly luminescent.

He wondered if they looked that way all the time or if it was just because she was drunk.

"Can I get another lemon drop?" she asked. She was holding up a nearly empty martini glass and looking right at him.

"Ask them," he suggested, nodding toward the bartenders. He lifted the hatch and stepped out from behind the bar.

She took a few steps toward him, tottering slightly on the high-heeled shoes she wore. They were just as red and glittery as her sweater. "But I asked you."

"And I don't work here." Which should be obvious considering the tool bag and all. He glanced at the group of people she'd been with, but none of them seemed to be giving her a lick of attention. Instead, they were all focused on the gold beach-ball-sized ornament covered in twinkling white lights that was suspended from a string in one corner of the bar.

It was the Colbys version of the New Year's Eve ball, and the countdown was clearly on.

One of the cocktail waitresses was standing on a chair near the ball, holding big cue cards over her head with a number printed on them. When the crowd shouted the number she held, she dropped the card to show another.

"...eight! Seven!"

"Keep up, Olivia," someone shouted. "You're dragging."

The waitress laughed. "This is Weaver time, Bubba," she shouted in return. "You know we make our own rules!" She dropped the card.

"...six!" En masse, the customers were all crowding closer toward the sparkling ball, making the wall of people between Mac and the exit even more solid. "Five!"

He resigned himself to wait.

The brunette was looking at her empty glass, as if she'd lost her best friend.

He leaned down toward her, getting a faint hint of perfume. Nothing heady. Nothing overdone. Just... interesting. "Cheer up." He had to raise his voice to be heard. "The year's almost done!"

"...four! Three!"

Her lashes lifted. Her eyes gleamed almost as much as the lights taped around the beach ball. "Hallelujah for small mercies." She tilted her head toward him, leaning closer to be heard as well.

"...two! One! Happy New Year!"

The bar went wild.

Confetti shot from every corner, showering the crowd with tiny bits of colored tissue while the strains of "Auld Lang Syne" blasted from the sound system.

Mac eyed the brunette.

She had bits of blue and green clinging to her hair. A pink piece of confetti on her nose. All around them people were either kissing each other or singing.

Her eyes met his and something inside him shrugged.

"Happy New Year," he said and leaned down to brush his mouth lightly against hers.

Not quite as briefly as he'd intended. Not with

the way her lips suddenly fused to his, her fingers lightly pressing against his chest as she stretched up, following as he started to straighten away from her.

Confetti was still floating in the air around them when their lips finally parted.

In reality, only seconds had passed.

Still, it was enough to jar his pulse out of its usual rhythm.

She was staring up at him, her slightly unfocused eyes wide until another piece of confetti landed on her cheek. Then she blinked slowly. Those long lashes lowered, then came up again to reveal a wet sheen.

He figured that was more likely because of her inebriation than a result of a brief, meaningless kiss. "I'm sorry," he said anyway.

Her eyebrows drew together. "For what?"

Who knew? Whatever made a pretty woman's eyes fill with tears these days. He was thirty-eight years old and no closer to understanding the rules of women now than he'd ever been. The last time he'd taken a woman out on a proper date and held out the chair for her at dinner, she'd snapped at him that she didn't appreciate his paternalistic attitude.

There had not been a second date.

Kissing a stranger, even on New Year's Eve in a bar filled mostly with cowboys and cowgirls, was probably a hanging offense in comparison.

He looked over her head toward the group she'd been with earlier. And still, not a one seemed to be looking around to see where she'd gone.

He focused on her heart-shaped face again. On her huge hazel eyes. "What's your name?"

"Delia."

Someone bumped into her on their way toward the bar and he steadied her when she stumbled forward. "I'm Mac. You have a ride home, Delia?"

"Is that an offer? I'll take it."

It hadn't been an offer. Not for a ride or for anything else. "Be careful what you ask for, Delia." He dropped his hand from her shoulder and shoved it in his pocket. "You live here in town?" Weaver was pretty small. Not as small as Cradle Creek where he'd been raised, but it still didn't take long getting from one end to the other.

She nodded. "Outskirts."

That could mean anything. "You have a coat?"

She frowned slightly, looking around her as if it were likely to be lying around her feet somewhere.

He sighed faintly. "Stay here." He nudged her onto a chair that had been vacated during the big New Year's ball drop and got Charmaine's attention.

"You know her?" He jerked his head toward Delia.

"Delia? Sure. She comes in occasionally."

"She needs a ride home."

Charmaine rolled her eyes. "So do fifty percent of the customers here. Sheriff department's offering free rides later."

"Make sure she gets one of them, would you?"

"Come on, Mac. Last thing I want to do is baby-sit—"

He pulled out his wallet and handed her a bill. "Or

at least make sure she doesn't leave here with some-one you don't know and trust."

She considered it for a moment. "I know and trust you. Why don't you take her home?"

"Because she's drunk and I'm a stranger to her and she's got no business getting into my truck for that reason alone. Plus with my luck, she'd pass out or puke." He'd dealt with both, but it'd been a long day and he wasn't in the mood.

"You think *I* want someone passing out or puk-ing in *my* car?"

"All right then, consider it a favor."

She looked stymied for a moment, then her lips twisted. "Give that Jackson a twin and I'll drive her home myself."

He pulled out the second bill. "Throw in a bowl of chili and a couple coffees to go."

Charmaine snatched the money from his fingers and tucked it in her back pocket. He didn't blame her. She had two kids at home that she had to feed. Kids he knew well since he'd caught one of them break-ing into his garage once.

Ethan hadn't gotten away with it and Mac hadn't pressed any charges. Instead, he'd ended up teaching the kid about auto mechanics. That was two years ago and since then Ethan had been joined by his sis-ter Carmela as well as a dozen more teenagers who'd been directed Mac's way by the sheriff.

After Charmaine handed him the food and cof-fee, he returned to Delia and set one of the cups on the table in front of her.

She eyed the to-go cup. "Is that coffee?"

"Yes. And you can drink it. Charmaine's going to give you a ride home."

Her hair bounced around her shoulders as her head whipped up to look at him. "Excuse me?"

"She's the bartender with the red braids."

"I know who Charmaine is!"

"Good." He dropped a couple of packaged sugars and creamers on the table next to the coffee cup. "Happy New Year, Delia."

Then he turned for the door while he still had the good sense to go.

Chapter Two

"Your grandmother is waiting for you."

Delia looked up at the bald man standing in the doorway to her bedroom suite. She'd been up for more than two hours, yet her head was still pounding so unmercifully she'd promised herself she would never have a cocktail again. "Ever heard of knocking, Montrose?"

He just stared down his nose at her.

Delia had no idea how old he was. He walked as slow as death, but he was tireless when it came to fulfilling his duties. Technically, he was her grandmother's chef. But in reality, he handled every detail involved in running the gigantic house.

His suit was black and severe, and the white cravat tied under his turkey neck was pristine. The attire wasn't even because of the special New Year's Day brunch.

He dressed the same way every day.

"The rest of her guests have already arrived," he intoned.

In other words, *she* was late.

"You know me, Montrose. Why be on time when there's an entrance to be made?"

His disapproving expression didn't change. He merely departed with his usual ponderousness.

Delia rolled her eyes at his back.

But she followed him, smoothing down her thigh-length sweater dress and wishing she could just crawl back into bed. Focusing blindly on the back of Montrose's bald head, she prayed the aspirin she'd taken would kick in soon.

Like Delia, Montrose lived at Vivian Archer Templeton's mansion. He'd worked for her in Pennsylvania and several years ago when she'd decided to move to Weaver, she'd coaxed him out of retirement and into moving there too. He was condescending and stuck up and was an endless annoyance to Delia, but he held a real job in the mansion whereas Delia's stint as Vivian's "personal assistant" was something far more trumped up.

Delia was thirty-four years old. In comparison to her over-accomplished siblings and cousins, she was absolutely the dullest knife in the drawer. Thus the pity job working for the eccentric, rich granny she'd never even known existed until five years ago.

And now, enduring the worst hangover she'd had

in a long while, she had the pleasure of attending her grandmother's New Year's Day brunch. Alone.

All because her last-ditch effort the night before at Colbys to find a date for it had been one gigantic failure.

Which just showed how much logic she had. Going to a bar on New Year's Eve where everyone was already paired off.

Instead of finding that date—someone who could at least pretend to be interested in her for a few measly hours—she'd drunk too much and been rejected by the only presentable male who hadn't already had a partner by his side.

The humiliation burning inside her over that detail was stingingly fresh.

Now that it was too late anyway, she realized she'd have been better off trying her luck at Shop-World than at Colbys. Shop-World rarely closed and the people wandering the aisles on the last night of the year were probably as single as her.

Did Mac of the intensely blue eyes shop alone at Shop-World, too? Or did he have a wife? A girlfriend?

If he did, what the heck was he doing out kissing a stranger on New Year's Eve?

Thinking he might be a jerk was preferable to feeling rejected.

She'd had enough of that lately to float a sea of boats.

Lagging behind Montrose was a physical impossibility. The man walked too slowly for her not to catch up to him.

She gave him a smirk of a smile just for the sheer pleasure of it and sailed ahead of him into the formal dining room only to stop short.

Entering the room ought to have offered no surprises for her. She'd handled the invitation list for her grandmother's brunch. Or thought she had.

Instead of the one long table that Delia expected, there were two. Why hadn't Vivian told Delia she'd basically doubled the invitation list?

Maybe Vivian was finally tired of the whole personal assistant thing. Maybe she was finally going to cut her losses where Delia was concerned.

Maybe Delia didn't even care.

That thought clanged around inside her head as she surveyed the ridiculously long, crystal-laden tables and the four young servers wearing black clothes and white gloves who stood in the corners of the room. If it weren't for all the children also seated at the table, it would have looked like some royal re-enactment.

She'd become accustomed to her grandmother's sense of ostentation, but she still couldn't help feeling wary as she entered the room and aimed for her parents sitting midway along the nearest table.

She'd expected to see nearly all of Vivian's family there. Expected to see the business associates that had been on the invite list that Delia *had* known about.

What she didn't expect to see were so many relatives from the other side of Vivian's family—the people related to her late first husband, Sawyer Templeton.

Those relatives descended from Sawyer's half sister, Sarah, who had died long before Delia was born. Most of them had been to the mansion. Many times over. Vivian welcomed them as the family they were. And vice versa.

The same could not be said of their patriarch, Squire Clay. Sarah had been his first wife and he had absolutely no love for Vivian.

Yet there he sat.

At the far end of the tables, directly opposite Delia's grandmother. As disconcerting as his piercing ice-blue gaze was as he watched Delia enter the room, she preferred it over the pitying looks from some of the others.

She reached her parents and leaned down to kiss them both. "Happy New Year," she murmured.

"What's Squire doing here?" Her mother whispered even though it was unlikely anyone would overhear. Everyone except Vivian and Squire was busy talking.

Delia cast a sideways look toward her grandmother. "No idea," she whispered back. "At least I didn't see a shotgun by his side." She smiled weakly at Vivian, who was giving her a look equally as intent as Squire's.

Delia's chair was the only one not yet occupied. It sat adjacent to Vivian's as if Delia were her right hand.

A right hand that, apparently, didn't know what the rest of the body was doing at all.

She hurried past her family with a practiced smile and circled around Vivian. "Happy New Year, Vivvie." She bussed her grandmother's delicately lined cheek. "What kind of mischief have you cooked up for brunch?"

"Since you've finally graced us with your presence, you'll learn soon enough." Vivian pushed to her feet and launched into an effusive welcome.

Delia glanced along the table across from her. Her sister, Grace, was surreptitiously checking her cell phone. Two chairs down from her, one of Squire's grandsons, Casey, was quietly refereeing something between his twin daughters while his wife, Jane, was unsuccessfully shielding a smile with her hand.

Jane owned Colbys Bar & Grill.

Delia closed her eyes for a moment.

She didn't want to think too much about Colbys.

"As you know—" her grandmother hadn't lost a speck of steam "—my newest little project has almost come to fruition. The new Gold Creek Recreation Center will be as welcome an addition to our community as the Finley Memorial Library was last year. I trust I can count on all of you to join the celebration when we officially open next month."

Delia couldn't help glancing toward Squire. He sat on the town council and bucked against all of Vivian's "community" projects. But the man's expression was even more unreadable than usual.

"And of course," Vivian continued, "we can thank

my favorite architect, Nick Ventura, for his tireless efforts on both projects."

Delia clapped politely, following Vivian's lead. She was well aware that Nick would be present since he'd been on the list she'd worked on. He sat several chairs down on Delia's side of the table, with one arm around his new wife and the other filled with a blanket-wrapped bundle.

She *really* wished she'd been able to walk into this stupid brunch with a convincing date by her side.

Half the people there—if not all—knew that she'd had a thing for Nick. She could see people even now sliding looks from Nick and his happy little family toward her.

Even Mac had given her a pitying look the night before. A man she'd never seen before in her life. He had no way of knowing she'd wasted the last few years chasing a guy who'd been so disinterested he hadn't even entered the race.

Loser may as well have been tattooed on her forehead. Which was probably the reason he'd kissed her.

The only woman in the place who hadn't had someone to share a midnight kiss.

Feeling parched, she picked up the cut crystal flute filled with champagne and orange juice and took a long drink, letting Vivian's voice wash over her.

Her grandmother did love a good speech. Delia had become an expert at tuning out every other sentence.

"...and now that it's another new year, there's another new project that I know will surprise..."

Delia was glad it was a new year. She was *so* done with the old one. Done with unrequited crushes on nice-guy architects. Done with unrequited crushes, period.

Confetti caught in burnished blond hair swam in her mind and she tilted the flute, finishing off the last few ounces. It still didn't help the thoughts swirling in her clanging head, though.

She'd had too much to drink, but not enough to dull a single detail. Including Mac's high-handed way of organizing her ride home as if she were incapable of doing it herself.

"...and we both agree that infusing a million dollars a year..."

He'd even *paid* Charmaine to make sure Delia got home safely. Well, no thanks. She'd paid Charmaine another twenty with instructions to tell Mac just where he could put his money. She'd left her car parked in the lot and gone home in the front of a sheriff's car.

Delia's car was still parked at the bar. Maybe she'd have her parents drop her off at Colbys once the brunch was over. The place was closed for the holiday. She wouldn't need to worry about running into blue-eyed strangers who figured she didn't have sense enough not to drink and drive.

Her stomach growled suddenly, and she gave a sideways look at the tiered arrangement of pastries an arm's length away. Montrose annoyed the stuffing out of her, but he made the most delicious palmiers. But she didn't dare reach for one just yet. Not because he was standing at the alert nearby, but because even she wasn't rude enough to begin eating while her grandmother was still yammering on.

"...my dear Arthur believed in helping others..."

Delia wanted to groan. Once Vivian started talking about "dear Arthur," she could very well go on for days. Vivian had buried four husbands and Arthur Finley had been the last. And to hear her tell it, he'd been the love of her life.

It made for a good story. The rich Pennsylvania-society widow who'd married a public schoolteacher.

Delia wasn't a widow. She wasn't a society-anything. And she certainly wasn't rich. But at the rate she was going, it might take her until she was seventy before she met someone remotely like the love of her life.

"...and heading up the joint foundation will be our very own Delia."

More clapping. Delia joined in even as she belatedly realized she'd heard her own name. She looked toward Vivian, who had finally taken her seat, a supremely satisfied look on her face.

"Delia! Why didn't you tell us?"

Her attention swerved over to her parents. They were both looking at her with shock.

In fact, that was pretty much the expression on everyone's face.

And not all of it was directed her way.

A good portion was aimed at Squire Clay.

"Why didn't you tell us?" Casey asked him.

"Does Gloria know?"

Delia looked at Nick, who'd risen to his feet as he asked the question of Squire. Gloria was Squire's estranged wife and Nick's grandmother.

But Squire merely pushed to his feet and the room went silent.

Delia realized that she wasn't the only one holding her breath. The entire room seemed to be as well.

Squire picked up his champagne flute. "Vivian." His tone was short, but no more so than usual. "We have our disagreements—" someone in the room snorted "—but we're in complete agreement when it comes to Delia."

"To Delia." Vivian picked up her champagne flute as did everyone else. Everyone else who hadn't already drunk the contents the way that Delia had, that is.

"To Delia," they echoed.

She managed a weak smile.

What the *hell* had she missed?

Chapter Three

"Appreciate you opening up like this, Mac. Last thing I expected was a flat tire on New Year's day."

"No problem, Squire." Mac finished tightening a lug nut on the tire he'd just replaced. "Always have time for your business. You know that by now."

"Fortunate, I suppose, that it happened nearby and not while I was out at the Templeton place."

"Vivian Archer Templeton's?" Mac glanced curiously at the old man. Calling the woman's enormous estate a "place" was something only a man who owned one of the largest cattle ranches in the state could pull off.

"Had to go out there for *brunch*." He said the word as if it was distasteful.

"Probably better than my oatmeal," Mac said humorously.

"Yeah, I'll give you that. Food was good." Squire resettled his cowboy hat. "Mostly it was something that needed doing."

The man didn't elaborate and Mac didn't ask him to.

Finished with the lug nuts, he carried the spent tire outside the bay door and tossed it in the trailer. When it was full, he'd have Cadell or Toby haul it to the recycler. They were both still apprenticing and were always looking for a reason to get out of the garage.

Assuming Mac didn't fire Toby before then. He was still aggravated about the stunt the kid had pulled the day before and if he didn't know how much Toby's mom depended on him, Mac would have canned him on the spot.

Taking a customer's car out for a joy ride was not okay. Leaving it abandoned in a parking lot was not okay.

Trying to lie his way out of it when Mac had found out was particularly not okay.

It was the lie that infuriated Mac the most. He'd thought they'd gotten past that stage a long time ago.

He went back inside.

Squire was leaning against the truck. "Time was I'd'a changed my own tires." He squinted into the distance. "Helluva thing getting old. Guess it beats the alternative, though, don't it?"

"It's what my mother tells me." The old man

looked tough as shoe leather and stood as tall as
Mac. Age hadn't stooped him any, whether he was
changing his own tires anymore or not. And the
Clays kept Mac in damn good business. Not just
with their personal vehicles but a lot of the Double-
C ranch ones, too.

There wasn't any excuse for Toby's stunt, but at
least he hadn't gone joy riding in a Double-C truck.
Everyone and their mother's brother recognized the
brand printed on the door of their vehicles.

He pushed away his annoyance with Toby again.
Mac had done the right thing warning Toby not to
show his face around the garage for the next few
days.

"Got special plans for the rest of the day, Squire,
or was brunch pretty much it?"

The old man's lips twisted a little. "Granddaughter's expecting everyone all up at their place later
this afternoon."

He had a lot of granddaughters. Grandsons.

When it came to living in Weaver, a person had
a good chance of running into one relation or another of Squire Clay's just by turning around on the
sidewalk.

"Angel's Flight," the older man continued, naming the new resort that had opened on Rambling
Mountain. "All the work April and Jed put into getting it built with that Stanton fella, can't blame 'em
for wanting to show it off."

Didn't sound to Mac like Squire was any more

enthusiastic about seeing the show than he'd been about brunch.

"Jed was in the other day," he said. Picking up a part he'd asked Mac to order. Unless it was something complicated, Jed Dalloway didn't mind getting his hands greasy. "Mentioned the work was finally done on his and April's cabin."

"Ever see it when Otis Lambert was still alive?"

Mac shook his head. "No, but Jed was telling me about it. Shared a brochure on Angel's Flight, too." It was sitting around somewhere.

"Wasn't nothing but a one-room shack when Otis Lambert owned it," Squire said. "Now it's a real nice log-cabin style place."

According to the brochure, Lambert's small ranch had been turned into a luxury resort, providing Angel's Flight guests with a dude ranch experience in the bargain. The rest of Lambert's land had been turned into a state park that had more than doubled the number of visitors to the area. "Sounded like they were glad to be moving back into it."

"Yep. Yep. Person likes their own home." Squire settled his hat again. "Ought to anyhow."

He seemed in no hurry to go.

Didn't bother Mac any. "Have coffee on in the office. Get you a cup?"

The man looked like he might agree. Then he shook his head. "I'll let you get to it. Y'oughta have plans of your own."

"Only thing waiting upstairs for me is the football game I'm recording," he admitted. "That and a bowl of chili from Colbys."

"Need yourself a girl, Mac. Best way to start off a new year is with a good woman at your side."

Mac chuckled. "Hell, Squire, I'm too busy to find the time." Dewy hazel eyes drifted into his mind. He'd spent way too much time thinking about the woman from the night before. "Might take some of that advice for yourself, though." He knew the old man and his wife, Gloria, had been having troubles for some time now.

The old man squinted into the distance again. "I'm working on it, Mac. I'm working on it." Squire clapped him on the shoulder and then turned to climb into the truck. "Put the tire on the account."

"Will do." The Clay account alone had allowed Mac to enclose four more bays on the back side of the garage. If Squire had wanted the tire for free, Mac would have given it to him.

He stepped out of the way and Squire backed out of the bay and drove across the parking lot, sketching a salute out the window before turning onto Main Street.

Mac reached up for the chain to pull down the bay door.

He looked into the distance, wondering if he saw the same things that Squire Clay had.

In one direction, a horizon of ranchland in the shadow of a mountain.

In the other direction, a town whose boundary crept closer every day.

When Mac had taken over his uncle's business, the garage had been a full mile beyond the furthest outskirts of Weaver. The only thing out that way besides Rasmussen Automotive had been the abandoned building across the street. It had been home to a video rental store and a barbershop. The striped pole had still been hanging on the side of the building.

Now, just five years later, he had an all-night convenience store next to him and a neighborhood of houses trying to grow up around him while across the street, a construction zone was turning the abandoned building into a new recreation center.

Mac's garage now *was* the outskirts of town.

He pulled on the chain and closed the door.

Chapter Four

What had she missed?

Four hours after her grandmother's brunch-time announcement and Delia was still trying to catch up.

She stared at her grandmother where she sat in her favorite chair in the conservatory—a glass-walled, tropical plant-filled room that was about as practical here in the middle of Wyoming as lipstick was on a pig. But everything about the lavish home that Vivian had built smack in the middle of cattle country was incongruous. "Have you *lost* your mind?"

Vivian dashed an imaginary speck away from her slacks. Once the guests were gone, she'd exchanged her vintage Chanel suit for silk palazzo pants and a cashmere sweater—her version of weekend casual. But the heavy diamonds on her frail-looking fingers were ever the same. "My mind is as fit as always despite the tumor squatting in my skull, if that's what you're worried about. Until I've redeemed myself, instead of finally joining Arthur, I'm afraid you're all still stuck with me."

Delia propped her hands on her hips and glared. She hadn't changed at all because she'd been too busy fielding comments about her surprising turn of fate. "I wasn't worried." Vivian's tumor was small and hadn't caused any new ill effects in several years. But she was in her late eighties. Everyone in Delia's family expected her to keep a close eye on her grandmother. It was the one thing they trusted her to accomplish.

She threw herself down on the cushioned chair across from Vivian and raked her fingers through her hair. "And I wish you'd stop talking about dying," she said flatly. "You're stubborn enough to outlive us all."

"And I'm stubborn enough to stick with our decision."

"*Our* decision." Delia pounced on that. "You and Squire *detest* each other. But the two of you are kicking in twenty million to fund this thing? If you want to give away money, you could just walk down Main Street in Weaver and toss it in the air. It'd be a lot easier!"

"Squire detests *me*," Vivian corrected. "And not without cause. When Sawyer discovered Sarah was his sister, I treated her abominably. She was illegitimate. I actively tried to prevent her from being acknowledged as a Templeton. Back in those days, these things mattered, or seemed to matter and I treated her as though she was a criminal rather than a victim of her circumstances." She folded her arms. "But that does not erase *his* behavior in the years since. Squire's always been irritating and stuck in his ways, but evidently not as much as I thought. When he approached me about establishing—"

"Wait. *He* approached you? This debacle is his idea? When? Why?"

"Several months ago." Vivian studied the rings on her hand.

"And you didn't say anything until today?"

"It's taken this long to get the legalities of establishing a joint foundation in place. As to why? His reasons are his own for wanting to bury the hatchet."

Delia squinted, feeling a horrifying suspicion take form. Squire and his wife had separated more than a year ago. And according to Delia's dad, Vivian liked acquiring husbands. Since she'd had four, was she looking for a fifth? "You're not involved… romantically…with him are you?"

Vivian actually snorted. "With that judgmental old cowboy? Surely you know me better than that. No one can follow in Arthur's footsteps. Least of all a boor like Squire Clay. He has his reasons. I have mine. Let's leave it at that."

"Okay, fine. But putting me in charge of running this thing is something else entirely!"

"How many times must I explain?"

"Until you realize your explanations don't make sense!"

"They make perfect sense. We will be a board of three. Me. Squire, heaven help me. And you. Our roles will be to ensure the foundation's perpetuity. Your role will be to ensure the mission of the foundation is followed."

She felt like tearing out her hair. *"What's the mission?"*

"We haven't entirely agreed on that. Regardless, it won't be complicated, Delia. Every year you'll award a certain percentage of the total funds. This first year, it'll be a million. That entails periodically reading a few grant proposals and deciding whether to fund them. It's not as if you'll be in charge of managing the principal. We have financial firms handling all of that."

"I'm not that naïve, Vivian. There's still got to be more to it."

"Details," Vivian dismissed. She picked up her cup and saucer and on cue Montrose appeared with the teapot. He refilled the cup and disappeared out the doorway again.

If Delia didn't know better, she'd think there were hidden cameras around the place that he monitored just so he'd know when he was needed.

Delia picked up her can of soda and noisily sucked at the straw until it was empty. "If this is some sort of ploy to improve your relationship with Daddy or Uncle Carter, it's not going to work."

"This isn't about David or Carter."

Delia exhaled and shoved off the cushioned chair again. She paced to the wall of windows overlooking the rear of Vivian's expansive property and stared out at the gray landscape.

Be careful what you wish for, she thought.

She'd wanted a fresh start.

Evidently what she'd gotten was a fresh start on her next failure.

Given the stakes, it would be a monumental one.

"I have a lot of money," Vivian said after a moment. "This is one of several small steps to ensure it does more for this world than pile up uselessly."

Delia could see the ten million from Vivian easily. That was almost commonplace. But she was surprised about Squire. She'd known the Double-C was huge. But she'd had no idea he had that sort of money at his fingertips. "This is just another one of your constant efforts to live up to Arthur's expectations, isn't it." It wasn't a question.

"He was a good man. I wish all of you would have had a chance to know him."

"And you're a good woman! Or he wouldn't have chosen you!"

"I wasn't always." Vivian suddenly looked tired. "If I'd have been a better mother—" She broke off and shook her head. "First Thatcher ran off when he was only eighteen to get away from me because he still blamed me for his father's death. Even after he died, he succeeded in hiding the life he'd made. A child of his own—" She pressed her lips together again and cleared her throat.

Thatcher, Delia knew, had died when he was still a young man.

But now, Thatcher's son was a grown man who had come forward the summer before to introduce himself and his family to his grandmother. Technically, Delia and Gage Stanton were related. But she had exchanged maybe a dozen words with him in the time since.

Mostly, she just knew that *his* wife happened to be best friends with Nick's new wife, Megan.

"Put Gage in charge. He's a real estate developer. A businessman. He won't make a mess of things."

"Gage doesn't need my help."

"Then Archer." She named another cousin—one much closer to home. "Or Nell. They're both lawyers."

"We've put you in charge, Delia." Vivian's voice was flat. "Get used to it and stop wailing. It's unbecoming."

Delia paced back to the windows and looked out again. "Ever think it's unbecoming to toss a person into a situation they're entirely incapable of handling? I'll humiliate us all."

"Now you're just being dramatic. You're capable of more than you think. But," Vivian raised her hand, "I don't expect you to figure all this out on your own. Stewart Junior will be here to guide you at first. He's coming to town next week. Montrose is preparing the guesthouse for him."

Delia slowly turned on her heel. *"Stewart St. James?"* She'd met her grandmother's attorney a few times while accompanying her to the Templeton compound back in Pennsylvania. And he was almost as old as Vivian. "You've convinced him to move to Weaver, too?"

"Stewart *Junior*. Really, Delia. You must learn to listen better."

Delia went still for a moment. She remembered meeting the son once. Tall, dark, handsome. A bit older than her. Kind of uptight for her tastes but she'd thought that about most everyone at one time or another. "How long's he staying?"

"As long as it takes to get you settled."

"Be easier if you'd just put him in charge and save us all the trouble."

"I expect you to be pleasant to the man," Vivian said. "He's doing this as a personal favor."

"I'll be pleasant." She controlled the urge to roll her eyes. "So where's this foundation supposed to operate from anyway? Have you been secretly designing another new building with Nick? The library and Gold Creek weren't enough for you?"

"There's no new building," Vivian said equably. "Ultimately, where you wish to set up an office is your choice but I'm glad you mentioned Gold Creek since I'm depending on you to also oversee the details of its opening—"

"*What* details?"

"Don't act alarmed. You were always going to handle the grand opening party anyway—"

"Yeah, a *party*." Unless there was a blizzard, it would be a success just because people always showed up when they knew there'd be free food and music. "Just a party."

"Well, now you can add filling the remaining staff positions as well so there can even *be* an opening. Stewart will be of great assistance on that score, too. You'll need to start with a manager first, since Marty Wells has dropped the ball on us by quitting even before we've opened."

Her headache was mounting. She didn't know anything about hiring employees. "Marty only quit because he had to go take care of his mother in Florida."

"Anyway, as I was saying, since you'll be attending to matters at Gold Creek, it would be logical to also conduct your foundation business there as well. Choose whichever office you like. Or continue using your regular office right here or set up camp in one of Squire's dusty barns. I really don't care. And Squire doesn't give a fig about it." She waited a beat. "Did you get a chance to admire Nick and Megan's baby? I was pleased that they came," she added, filling the stony silence. "I wasn't sure they would, since little Robin isn't even a month old yet."

There was only so much a person could take.

Delia picked up the soda can and carried it with her out of the conservatory.

She stomped down to Montrose's kitchen, threw the can in the compactor and jumped a foot when he appeared around the corner.

"Don't disappoint your grandmother."

She grimaced. "Interestingly enough, Montrose,

that's what I'm trying *not* to do." Knowing it would annoy him no end, she yanked open the commercial-sized refrigerator and stared blindly at the rigidly organized contents. "I suppose she told *you* about this foundation business with Squire Clay?"

"A few days ago when she saw fit to tell me the guest list for today had doubled. And that—if I needed help with the preparations—she could call on *Bubba Bumble*." He said the name with disdain.

Delia bit back a smile. Bubba Bumble was the cook at Ruby's Diner whom Vivian had been known to hire occasionally. Not just because he was a terrific cook, but because the rival chef got under Montrose's skin.

He pushed her aside, reached inside the refrigerator and handed her a bottle of the pressed juice that she favored. "Don't toss her offer back in her face. She deserves better."

Delia's shoulders slumped.

Montrose was at his most annoying when he was right.

Chapter Five

Mac saw the red car speed down the road past his garage and shook his head slightly.

He'd lost count of how many times he'd seen the same car going and coming. It wasn't usually speeding. Much. But there was a turn in the road up ahead that could get the best of sturdier vehicles on a good day.

Today was not a good day.

One month into the new year and winter was on a roll. He'd already hauled two cars out of the snow in the past week, and that was before the latest storm. It had started the night before and was still going strong.

He finished pulling down the rolling bay door and locked it, then glanced at the clock on the wall beside the tire rack. It was nearly two in the afternoon. Which meant he had less than a half hour to get cleaned up and over to the courthouse.

"Yo, Mac!"

He looked toward the long window separating the garage from the office area. Loreen Ruiz, his office manager was standing on the other side of it, hailing him over the loudspeaker. Even though they were the only two people there since he'd already sent Cadell and Toby home. Even though she could have walked two feet to the doorway and gotten his attention that way.

That was just Loreen. Woman didn't take one step she deemed unnecessary. And she loved the loudspeaker.

She was also the best office manager he could have asked for. She'd worked at Rasmussen Automotive since Mac was a kid and if she'd felt so inclined, could outperform Cadell and Toby and any of the other mechanics who'd ever passed through its rolling doors.

He spread his hands, still waiting. "Yeah?"

"Casey Clay says he has a dishwasher at his house he's getting rid of if you know someone who needs it."

How on earth Mac had ended up being the go-to when it came to people getting rid of household appliances was still a mystery to him. "Anything wrong with it?"

"Didn't say."

"Tell him I'll try to swing by tonight."

"Roger." The loudspeaker crackled into silence and her head of dyed-black hair disappeared as she sat down at her desk.

Mac wiped his hands on the rag from his back pocket and reverently lowered the silver hood of the Rolls-Royce. The luxurious vehicle stuck out like a sore thumb around Weaver. Same as the mansion its owner had built. And if the rich old lady didn't drive the vehicle like a bat out of hell, he'd have gone his entire life without ever getting his hands greasy keeping a Rolls in tune.

But Vivian Archer Templeton did drive like a bat out of hell. Even a vehicle suitable for kings and queens didn't have a chance against the likes of her.

He polished a fingerprint off the gleaming finish and pocketed his rag once more before heading into the office. Aside from working on the Rolls, they'd spent the day cleaning up and organizing. The garage had been open all day, but every appointment had canceled because of the weather. Even Montrose, the bald guy who always dropped off and picked up the Rolls, hadn't come to retrieve the car.

"You might as well cut outta here," he told Loreen. "There's no reason for you to stay until closing time."

She was sitting at her desk, but she still managed to give him a look right down her nose. "Your bills don't get paid by themselves." She finished tearing a check from the big old-fashioned book of them as if to underscore her point. God forbid she learn to print the checks through the computer program designed for that very purpose.

He pulled the door closed behind him, keeping the warm air in. "I *am* the owner here. If I tell you to take off early, maybe you ought to just consider it. Toby and Cadell did."

She narrowed her eyes. "Compare me again to those boys and I might leave early and not come back."

He grinned. He'd learned a long time ago that her threats were mostly noise. "I'm gonna clean up and head over to the courthouse."

"There's no way the judge is going to give Charmaine's ex-husband shared custody of Carmela and Ethan. Eddie's never wanted any responsibility where they're concerned. And ever since Ethan's been in your Tuesday group, he's stayed mostly out of trouble, hasn't he? You going to have to make a statement about him?"

"If the attorney needs me to. And if the hearing's not postponed altogether." Weather like it was, anything was possible. "If *you* need me, you know where to find me."

Her scoffing *"please"* followed him out of the office. He ducked his head against the sting of wet, pelting snow and hurried up the stairs to his apartment.

Living above his place of work was both a convenience and a pain in the ass. It meant he was never late to work. But it also meant he was never away from work.

He showered and changed into clean jeans and

layered on a couple shirts and his coat before heading back out the door again.

Aside from one phone call concerning the hearing, he hadn't talked to Charmaine since New Year's Eve at Colbys.

He thought once again about the brunette from that night. Delia of the luminescent hazel eyes had been a frequent visitor in his dreams.

It would've been easy enough for him to find out more about her. He could have asked Charmaine. Hell, he could have asked Loreen. She'd lived in Weaver since the dark ages and knew every face in town.

But he hadn't looked for more information.

His life was busy enough already. He didn't have time for the complications that relationships always brought.

Then again, Delia hadn't exactly struck him as someone on the hunt for a relationship, either.

But the taste of her lips was still vivid in his mind a month later.

The sharp wind snapped him out of his reverie and he hurried down the rest of the stairs and back into the office.

"Snow's piling up fast out there," he told Loreen. He jangled his keys. "I think you should drive home now while you can. Seriously."

She angled back to look out the window to judge for herself. "If it gets too bad, I'll call David to pick me up. He's on duty this afternoon."

Mac hoped she would. Dave Ruiz was a deputy

with the sheriff's department. His SUV had four-wheel drive and a snowplow of its own.

He left and drove through the snow to the Weaver courthouse. The parking lot was nearly empty.

Didn't bode well for Charmaine's hearing.

When he went inside, though, a clerk was sitting as usual at the information desk, and she pointed him down the tiled hallway beyond a walk-through metal detector. "Room 150," she said.

He dumped his keys and cell phone in the bowl under the narrow-eyed glare of the guard and walked through the metal detector.

On the other side, the guard handed the bowl back almost grudgingly. "Phones need to be silenced in the courtroom," he warned.

Mac had plenty of experience with courtrooms. "Already is." He pocketed his belongings and headed up the empty corridor to room 150—a glorified number meaning the fifth and last courtroom in the building. He pulled off his coat and opened the door.

The small room held only a few occupants. The judge at her desk. Charmaine and her lawyer at one table. Her ex-husband and his lawyer at another.

Sitting on one of the benches behind their mom were Carmela and Ethan.

Mac tossed his coat onto the empty bench behind them and slid in after it. Carmela gave him a small smile. She was twelve years old and unlike her brother who hated school and anything to do with it, she was an avid student. "Hey Mac."

"How's it going?" He kept his voice low.

"Same as usual." Her nonchalance was belied by the pencil she drummed against the thick textbook on her lap.

Mac looked at her brother. "Ethan?" He was fourteen now. Dark-haired like their father. Mac liked to think he'd helped keep Ethan from wanting to ever break into anyone's business again.

"If they make us go and stay with him, I'm outta here," Ethan muttered under his breath. "No way I'll stick around for that. I got money saved. I can get to Mexico or—"

Mac bumped the boy's shoulder lightly with his fist. "That wouldn't solve much." He ought to know. He'd done his own share of running away when he'd been young and pissed off at what he considered the injustices in his world.

All he'd accomplished was worrying his mother when she'd already had enough on her plate trying to provide for him and his brothers.

At the front of the courtroom the attorneys were arguing, and Charmaine looked over her shoulder. Despite the debate going on between the lawyers, she gave her kids an encouraging thumbs-up before turning her attention forward again.

Mac had to give her credit for her ability to stay positive.

She had a sleazebag of an ex-husband who routinely dragged her into court for one reason or another to fight for shared custody of the kids he'd abandoned as toddlers. His latest was the claim that Charmaine wasn't properly supervising Ethan, who'd managed to break his leg after sneaking onto a ski run up at Angel's Flight.

Fortunately, the judge didn't look particularly swayed by it at all and after nearly an hour—including a statement from Mac about Ethan's continuing participation in Mac's auto shop program plus written statements from his teachers at school—she finally banged her gavel. "I'll render my decision before the fifteenth of the month."

It wasn't the quick dismissal that Mac knew Charmaine had been hoping for. And obviously not the immediate result that Eddie had wanted. He stormed out.

His attorney offered an apologetic look and followed.

Charmaine's attorney left, too, and Charmaine stood and faced them. "All right," she said with forced brightness. "Mac, you want to join us for pizza?"

"Appreciate the offer but I need to get back to the garage." He picked up his coat and held open the courtroom door for them. "You might want to call ahead and make sure the pizza place is open. The snow—" He stared at the woman exiting the courtroom opposite theirs.

His dreams hadn't exaggerated her looks.

Her dark hair gleamed around her shoulders.

The sweater this time was ivory and just as closely fitted.

The jeans hugging her hips were ivory too.

Her lips were glossy red and though she wasn't laughing, Mac could hear it inside his head all the same.

Delia seemed to stop short at the sight of him, too. Then her hazel gaze moved from him to Charmaine and from Charmaine to the kids.

Her expression cooled noticeably.

She gave them a brief nod and tossed her off-white scarf over her shoulder before slipping her arms into the long black coat held out by the tall guy accompanying her. Then she tucked her hand through his crooked elbow as they walked swiftly up the vacant corridor. "Thank you again for this, Stewart. I'd have never convinced the judge without your help." Her words floated back to them, plainly audible.

Mac was willing to bet Stewart had never gotten grease under his fingernails. He looked like he wore his three-piece suit morning, noon and night.

"That reminds me." Charmaine fumbled with her purse. She pulled out two folded bills. "I never did give Delia that ride home. She insisted on using one of the sheriff's rides."

He grimaced and waved off the forty bucks. "Consider it my contribution toward your celebration pizza."

"If you don't want it, I'll take it." Ethan reached for the money.

"Get over yourself," Charmaine said tartly and tucked the money back inside her purse as they started their way up the hallway, too. She looked at Mac again. "Guess you've heard about that new job of hers."

He watched Stewart briefly touch Delia's back as

they circled around the metal detector. "I don't know what her *old* job is."

Charmaine gave him a resigned look. "The whole town's been talking about it since the article in *The Weaver Gazette* last month. She's in charge of that new charitable foundation of her grandmother's. Now everyone's wondering how they can get a piece of the fortune she'll be giving away for themselves."

"Not everyone," he said dryly. He never read the *Gazette*. "Who is her grandmother?" They passed the guard at the metal detector, who brushed past Mac to reach the door first and open it for Charmaine with a smile.

"Vivian Archer Templeton. Delia lives with her." She followed her kids to their parked car. "Sure I can't talk you into pizza?"

"I'm sure. Be careful driving." He waited long enough to know her car started okay before heading toward his truck.

The cab was bitterly cold as he thumbed the phone and the Bluetooth system he'd installed took over.

Loreen answered on the second ring. "I left you a message that I was home," she started off.

"I got it. What do you know about Vivian Templeton? Besides the fact that she's merciless on her Phantom."

"Why're you so interested all of a sudden?"

"Heard she's started up some new foundation." It was sort of the truth. "Was curious about it."

"Not just Vivian. Squire Clay's thrown in with her, too. Bonnie from my Bunko group thinks there's

something going on there between the two of them."
Loreen was clearly warming to the subject. "You
know Bonnie used to volunteer at the library—the
old one—along with Gloria Clay."

He didn't know. Much less care. "So?"

"Well, you *know* Gloria and Squire have been
separated for months. It's just a matter of time before the big D-I-V—"

"About the foundation?"

"According to the paper, they're giving money
away to—hold on. I've got it online here." He could
hear her keyboard clattering. "There it is. To support
our neighbors," she quoted. "Whatever that means.
If you ask *me*, it's all probably some way to avoid
paying taxes."

"Who's in charge of it?"

"Delia Templeton. And I can tell you, *that's* a
story that didn't get put in the paper. My neighbor
remembers teaching her in high school. Over in
Braden? Says she barely managed to graduate because she was more interested in goofing off than
studying. Now here she's in charge of something important like this?" Loreen tsked. "Just goes to show
that being an heiress comes in handy. She'd never
get a job like that otherwise. Are you thinking about
trying to get some money for the Tuesday troop of
troublemakers?"

"They're not troublemakers," he said irritably.
"And maybe I *am* thinking about it." He hadn't been,
but with some extra money, he could afford having
more than one group of kids. And it was better than

explaining that it was Delia herself that he'd really been interested in. "I've gotta go. Someone's calling on the shop line." It was an excuse but there was no way for Loreen to know that. Whenever the garage was closed, the phone line automatically transferred to his cell. "If you need a ride in the morning, let me know." He hung up before she could say anything else.

He sat there drumming his thumb on the steering wheel.

Delia was the rich lady's granddaughter.

Even more reason why he should be glad there'd been nothing more than a New Year's Eve kiss between them.

Loreen had said it.

Delia was an heiress.

Mac was a mechanic.

End of story.

Chapter Six

"There's the tow truck." Stewart pointed at the flashing yellow lights coming toward them on the highway. "Finally." He looked at Delia. "Are you *sure* you don't want to go to the hospital?"

Delia held her coat tighter around herself. "The only thing that might need a hospital is my car."

"Look, I'm sorry about—"

"I'm not blaming you."

Much.

The deputy sheriff had trained his SUV spotlight on the ditch, and she looked down at her poor car. The Porsche was ten years old. She'd bought it used. It wasn't entirely practical. But it was red and sporty, and she loved it.

And now, thanks to Stewart, it was more than nose-deep in snow. Down a ditch.

So what if she'd drained her savings account to pay it off? The salary that came with her new job would allow her to build it back up again soon enough.

As long as her grandmother and Squire Clay didn't come to their senses and put someone else in charge of their new venture who was actually qualified for the task.

It was her fault.

After the courthouse, she and Stewart had gone to dinner at a new restaurant on the other side of town and after, she'd handed over the keys to Stewart. Let him drive. She knew he'd been wanting to. She couldn't blame him. The Porsche was fun to drive. Then they'd hit the curve at mile post nine. It was tricky. Iced up easy.

At least neither one of them had gotten hurt.

She *was* grateful for that fact. Even though looking at her car now made her want to cry a little.

She snugged her scarf up around her chin and watched the tow truck driver swing down out of the high cab. He directed another bright spotlight toward the ditch and started climbing down toward the car, a long cable trailing after him.

He was dressed for the weather better than they were. Thick coat. And the ubiquitous cowboy hat worn by ninety percent of the local population was missing in favor of a thick cap pulled low over his head.

"Finally," Stewart said again, as if they'd been

waiting hours for the rescue when it had really been less than thirty minutes.

She stomped her feet again and looked at Dave Ruiz as the deputy approached them.

He had a clipboard in his hand, and he pulled off the top sheet. "Copy of the report," he said. "In case you need it for insurance purposes."

"Thank you." Delia took the paper, folded it and stuck it in her pocket.

"I don't think the car is damaged," Stewart said. "We couldn't get enough traction to get out of the ditch."

"Probably right, sir." Deputy Ruiz cleared his throat. "Ah... I, uh—" He cleared his throat a second time.

She glanced at him. "Is there something else you need, Deputy?"

He looked grateful for the opening. "Nothing I need, ma'am. I just wanted to say I saw the story in the *Gazette*."

Of course he had. Everyone had.

She couldn't help sliding a look toward Stewart. When he'd arrived in Weaver three weeks ago, his first act of business as her "advisor" was putting out a press release about her spearheading the collaboration between Vivian and Squire.

"You're really gonna give away a million dollars?" the deputy asked. "Just like that?" He snapped his gloved fingers.

"Broadly, yes," Stewart answered. "Each year. Not just to one person, of course."

She figured it was only fair that he got to explain. The *Gazette* piece had been *his* doing.

"And only if their need for funding falls within the general focus areas the foundation establishes," he was saying.

The deputy squinted slightly. "Focus areas?"

"Education, for example," Stewart said.

"Ah. You mean scholarships."

"And other things. All that has to be determined still."

"And anyone can apply."

"We're not at a stage to accept grant proposals. But yes, if certain requirements are met, anyone will be able to apply. Meanwhile, a temporary website has been established for inquiries."

Delia looked at the deputy. "Visit the website and fill in the form," she said, cutting to the chase. He'd be behind three hundred and seventeen others who'd already done so. "Describe what you need and as soon as we have more details, someone will be in touch."

Someone being her.

He'd pulled out a small notepad and had his stubby pencil ready. "What's the website?"

"WEAVERFUNDS."

He wrote down the name with all seriousness and pocketed the notepad. "I'd better get some of the traffic we're holding up moving." He jogged across the road where the flares he'd set earlier were still burning.

She looked back to see the progress on her car.

The tow truck driver had it hooked up to the cable and was climbing up the side of the ditch again.

The glare of the lights caught him in the face as he looked their way.

Even with the knit cap pulled low over his brow, she recognized his angular face.

Mac.

For the second time that day.

She looked toward the tow truck as if she expected to see Charmaine pop her head out. The cab was empty.

He reached his truck once more and the winch whined as it began to slowly turn. The cable went tight, and her car slowly appeared, rear bumper first.

He pulled the car all the way out onto the road while the deputy—emergency lights still flashing on the top of his SUV—directed the few passing cars to the far side of the road.

Mac unhooked the cable and retrieved a tool from his truck that he used to dislodge enough of the snow packed around the car so he could open the driver's door. He ducked his head and disappeared inside.

Stewart had left the key in the ignition and Delia could hear Mac trying to start the engine. It sputtered a few times but kept dying and he got back out and headed their way.

She realized she was holding her breath when he reached them. If he was as surprised by her presence as she was by his, he didn't show it. He just pulled off his knit cap, leaving his thick hair standing in spikes. His cheeks were ruddy from the cold. Comparing him to Stewart was like comparing steak to sushi.

They both had their merits, but she knew which one she preferred.

"Car won't start," Mac said, stating the obvious. "Might just be the snow." He looked from Stewart to Delia and back again. "I can tow her to the garage and take a closer look in the morning."

"That won't be necessary," Stewart said.

"Hold on. It's *my* car." She nodded toward the tow truck. "Rasmussen Automotive? That's where Montrose takes my grandmother's car."

Mac smiled briefly. "I can tow it anywhere else you want, too. Your decision. Wouldn't advise leaving it sit there, though."

"Rasmussen's is fine."

Mac's gaze finally moved away from Delia's face. He looked at Stewart. "Mac Jeffries." He stuck out his hand. "And you're...?"

Stewart hesitated. Only for a fraction of a second, but Delia noticed. Then he shook Mac's hand briefly. "Stewart St. James. I'm Delia's—"

"Business associate," she inserted quickly. "Deputy Ruiz offered to give us a ride earlier but he's on duty. I'm sure he has more important things to do. Would you mind taking us out to my grandmother's place?" She was simply being practical, she reasoned.

Something that Stewart had been coaching her about nonstop since he'd gotten here.

He wasn't giving her an approving look at all, though. In fact, he looked more uptight than Montrose on a good day.

"Do it all the time." Mac's deep voice was easy.

"Is there anything you need from inside the car?" He looked at both of them. "No? You'll be warmer waiting in the cab. Won't take me long to load her up."

He turned away and Delia started to follow, but Stewart caught her arm. "What do you know about this guy?" he asked in a low voice.

That he'd turned her down?

A month after the fact, she'd decided somewhere along the way that she was grateful for that. It meant one less thing to regret.

Even if his three-second kiss *was* still memorable.

"Mac works at the repair shop my grandmother uses for the Rolls. What else do I need to know?" She pulled away and continued toward the tow truck. Stewart came from the land of ride-share apps, but here in Weaver, you took a ride when you had one in hand. And unless it was an emergency, you didn't bother an on-duty deputy sheriff.

It was a high reach to climb up into the cab, but once she was inside, it was much warmer. She loosened her scarf as she slid to the center of the bench seat. Stewart climbed in beside her and a few minutes later, with her car loaded on the truck, Mac swung up behind the steering wheel.

It was cozy with all three of them sandwiched inside the cab.

But it was only Delia's left side that felt singed.

Mac put the truck in gear and they set off with a small lurch that knocked her shoulder against his.

"It's not far to my grandmother's house," she told him. "It's just a few miles—"

"I know where it is." His tone was bland. "Only one mansion around here."

She chewed the inside of her cheek. She didn't need to wonder any longer if he knew she was related to Vivian.

The silence in the truck cab was relieved by the faint crackle from the police radio attached to his dashboard and the rhythmic swish of his windshield wipers against the snow that fell in fits and spurts.

Those few miles had never felt so long and when he finally came to a stop on the brick courtyard in front of Vivian's house, Delia was grateful.

Stewart quickly climbed out and turned with his hand outstretched to help her down.

She didn't take it. "I'll be along in a second."

His lips thinned slightly but he nodded and headed toward the door.

Delia looked back at Mac. The same thing that had fluttered inside her chest on New Year's Eve fluttered again, and she couldn't even blame it on too many cocktails. "Thanks for the rescue."

"Next time don't drive so fast around that curve, and you won't need a rescue."

The fluttering plopped dead in the water. "*I* wasn't the one driving!"

She felt more than saw his gaze move past her to Stewart's departing form. "Too bad. Your date might have ended better without the ditch detour."

"It's not like that."

"Like what?"

He was looking at her again. Even in dim light his eyes were vividly blue.

She moistened her lips. "Stewart and I aren't... I mean, he's just here to—" She drew in a quick breath. What was it about Mac that made her feel so tongue-tied? "We weren't on a date. I told you. He's a business associate. My grandmother's the one who brought him here."

"Helping you give away this money I've been hearing about?"

"Gossip or *Gazette*?" The grapevine was arguably more effective than the free community paper.

"Only ever use the *Gazette* to line the cat box," he said.

She narrowed her eyes. "You have a cat?"

He shook his head. The corners of his lips twitched. "No."

She smiled and slid a few more inches along the seat toward the door, only to realize he was sitting on the long ends of her scarf. The more she moved, the more the scarf tightened around her neck. "I'm trapped."

"Guess I should move then."

Only he didn't.

That flutter was back again.

She tugged again on the scarf. Even she recognized it was a halfhearted effort at best.

She wanted to ask him why he'd been at the courthouse. How involved he was with Charmaine and her kids.

"So, I guess I'll just call you tomorrow," she said instead. "About my car?"

It was probably her imagination that his gaze dropped to her lips. They tingled anyway.

"I should be able to get to it first thing."

"You can add the cost of the tow and dropping us off—" She broke off when amusement crossed his face. "What?"

"Consider tonight a goodwill gesture." His eyes crinkled slightly.

"Your boss won't mind?"

His smile grew as he pulled a business card from his pocket and handed it to her along with the ends of her scarf. "Your grandmother sends us a lot of business. I'll let you know how much your car's gonna cost you."

She couldn't help a small laugh. "Oh, great. Be kind, please. *I* don't drive a Rolls." She slid the rest of the way across the seat and hopped down to the ground. "Thanks again." She pushed the door closed and stepped away while Mac pulled the truck around in a circle.

"Coming, Delia?"

She sighed faintly and looked toward Stewart standing in the doorway of the house. "I'm coming." She tapped the business card against her palm and joined him.

But she couldn't help one more glance over her shoulder at Mac's departing taillights before she went inside.

Chapter Seven

"You want the good news or the bad news?"

Delia tightened her grip on her phone at the sound of Mac's deep voice.

She'd waited until Montrose had cleared away the breakfast buffet before calling the number on the business card. Her grandmother hadn't come down for breakfast at all and Stewart had excused himself.

For the moment at least, she had the breakfast room to herself.

"I don't know," she said warily. "How bad is the bad?"

"Actually, everybody should be so lucky," he said. "You just need an alignment and a new headlight. Nothing serious."

She caught her reflection in the gilded mirror

hanging over the sideboard and wiped the goofy grin off her face. "If that's the bad news, then what's the good?"

"I can get the work done this morning."

"That is good news." She ran her fingertip around the perimeter of the business card. "I don't usually have that sort of luck. But other than all that, it's running again?"

"Like a top. Just try to avoid ditches and parking in snowbanks in general."

"I'll keep that in mind." She glimpsed at her reflection again and turned sideways in her chair to avoid it altogether. "When can I pick it up?"

"Any time after twelve. Need the address?"

"I managed not to lose your business card overnight," she said dryly. "See you then." Montrose entered the room as she ended the call. She set down her cell phone and watched him fuss about the room, restoring it to pristine order.

Today, his black suit was covered with a starched white apron and the white cravat had been replaced by a white bow tie. But as usual, he gave her no notice at all.

"Montrose, how long have you worked for Vivian?"

"I've worked for Madame since the dawn of time," he deadpanned and walked out of the room.

She followed him. "I'm serious. How long? Did you know dear Arthur?"

He turned into the kitchen. It was a huge room. Commercially designed to his exact specifications.

And he loathed allowing anyone in it, including her. "More than twenty-five years now. And yes, I knew Mr. Finley."

Twenty-five years was a long time, yet Delia had expected it to be longer. "Did you know her other husbands?"

"None that mattered," he said dismissively. He sat on a stool in front of the stainless-steel island and pulled the plastic wrap off the top of an over-sized bowl. "I never knew Mr. Templeton, if that's what you're asking." He scattered a circle of flour on the table, tipped the ball of dough out onto it and began kneading.

She watched his gnarled fingers for a moment. "Do you ever think about retiring again?"

He sighed loudly as if he were expending an immense amount of patience on her. "Yes. When you harangue me with pointless questions."

Always a pleasure, Montrose was.

She headed toward the doorway. "And just so you know, the poached eggs this morning were over-cooked." She escaped quickly but not before she heard the thud of the door slamming shut.

In the long run, she'd pay for the comment, but there was nevertheless something sweet in yanking the man's bow tie. Even though the poached egg on her Eggs Benedict had been divinely perfect.

As always.

There wasn't anything particularly unusual about Vivian not coming down for breakfast, but Delia stopped at her suite to check on her before heading to her own rooms on the opposite side of the house.

Her grandmother was sitting at her desk positioned near a window, writing letters. The old-fashioned kind on elegant parchment complete with tasteful monogram.

Delia eyed the small stack of already sealed envelopes sitting near her grandmother's elbow with some trepidation. "You're not writing every member of the town council to complain again, are you? What is it this time? The lack of proper public transportation?"

"There *isn't* proper public transportation in Weaver." Vivian glanced over the gold rims of her reading glasses. "When I met Arthur, he rode a bus every day to work. This town doesn't have a local bus route at all. And don't get me started on the school bus situation for the public schools."

"I'm sorry I mentioned it." She'd been half joking, for Pete's sake. "What's with the letters, then?"

Vivian precisely folded a sheet of letterhead and tucked it inside an envelope. "I'm planning a little soiree a couple weeks from Friday."

That was probably just as bad as taking the town council to task. Vivian did nothing without a motive. "Who is going to help you? Now that you've reassigned me to run the foundation, I mean. Are you going to advertise for an actual assistant?"

"You were an actual assistant." Vivian turned back to her letter writing.

"Not like Penny or Nell."

"The only person you need to compare yourself

against is you. But to answer your question, I'll hire another assistant when I find someone who suits me. I have no interest in advertising for one. And I don't need an assistant to pull off a little family party. Now, tell me how you're getting on with Stewart. I saw him walking to the guesthouse earlier."

"He said he had some calls to make." Delia sat on the arm of the settee. "And he's fine, I guess. He was useful at the courthouse yesterday." She picked up one of the fancy little pillows and toyed with the fringe. "I'd have never convinced Judge Bailey to cut the ribbon at the grand opening of Gold Creek. Not on my own." The image of Mac coming out of the other courtroom with Charmaine swam in her mind and she stuffed the pillow back in the corner of the settee.

"You had dinner with him last night. I assume that means you've finally forgiven him for the press release?"

She spread her hands. "I just think he could have let me know about it first. Even *I* could have predicted the way people would come out of the woodwork." Instead, she'd only learned about the release when she'd started receiving phone calls from people wanting to know how they could apply for the "free" money.

"In his defense, he didn't include your personal phone number. He very clearly indicated that inquiries could be sent to his firm. The *Gazette* editor is the one who added your cell phone number."

"And if Stewart had *forewarned* me, I could have

mentioned that Gerty Tomlinson has a habit of doing that sort of thing. Which would have been fine if we were talking about a bake sale!"

Now, the phone message on her phone directed people to just visit the website.

It hadn't stopped the incessant calls, but it had helped a little.

"I think he's learned his lesson," Vivian said. "He's here to guide. Not take over."

"Too bad. Even I'd be happy if he took over."

Vivian ignored that. "I'm sure he regrets your little accident last night."

"If I'm supposed to listen to his expertise, he ought to return the favor. At least *I* know where to speed and not to speed. I tried to warn him." Again, Mac's face swam inside her head, and she restlessly paced to the far side of the spacious suite. "Fortunately, there was no significant damage to the car."

"Fortunately, there was no significant damage to my granddaughter," Vivian returned mildly. "Or today would involve something very different than writing out invitations. You must agree he's quite handsome, though, don't you think?"

Burnished blond hair. A long jaw that was a little pointed and a lot stubborn. Plus those striking blue eyes… "Quite. *Wait*." She squinted at Vivian. "You mean Stewart?"

"Who else are we speaking about?"

Delia's neck felt hot. "Stewart is just here to keep me from falling on my face with this stupid job you've dumped on my head." She gave Vivian a stern look. "*Right?* No matchmaking."

Vivian folded her glasses and set them aside. "Do you really think the foundation is stupid, Delia?"

She exhaled noisily. "No, of course not." Her dad and sister were both physicians. Her brother was a military hero. None of them were in it for the accolades but because they genuinely believed in service to others. "But I still don't see why you've put me in charge of it all."

Vivian smiled slightly, clearly as unmoved now as she'd been every other time Delia had said the same thing. "One of these days, you'll thank me."

"Don't count on it, Vivvie," she groused. "But I still love you." She leaned to kiss her grandmother's cheek and saw Stewart striding back across the brick courtyard below the window. "I'd better get changed." She was still wearing the sweats and T-shirt she'd slept in. "We're finally interviewing people to replace Marty Wells this afternoon. Then we have a video meeting with a designer for the *real* website. So the sooner you and Squire can come to an agreement on what you even want to *name* the foundation, the sooner we can get a proper web address registered."

"As soon as we agree on something other than *WEAVERFUNDS*, you'll be the first to know." Vivian held out the envelopes. "I'd like you to hand-deliver these before the end of the week, please."

"As accustomed as I am to your idiosyncrasies," Delia fanned the stack, "what makes you think I have time to be running your personal errands these days?"

"Because I'm your frail grandmother and—"

"The grandmother part is correct," Delia said tartly. "But we both know frail is just an act."

Vivian's laughter followed her out the doorway.

Chapter Eight

"Sign at the bottom and you're good to go." Mac dropped the Porsche's key chain on the counter next to the work order outlining everything he'd done on her car.

Delia signed the form and took her credit card back from the woman—Loreen, according to the name plaque on the counter. "Thank you." She slid her card into her wallet and pretended she wasn't entirely distracted by Mac unzipping the front of his dark blue coveralls to reveal a snug white T-shirt and jeans underneath. "I appreciate how quickly you got it finished."

He'd pulled his arms out of the sleeves and left the upper half of the jumpsuit hanging around his hips. "It was rough." He jerked his thumb at the garage behind them. "Considering how slammed we are today."

Her car was the only one parked inside.

She smiled. "I still appreciate it." She followed him from the office into the cavernous space. It was very chilly and smelled like car tires but was scrupulously clean. Even the speckled floor was spotless. "Guess Montrose picked up the Rolls." She was certain he'd left early enough to avoid dropping her off at the garage at the same time. Instead, Stewart had done so.

"First thing this morning." He wiped his hands on a red rag before pulling open her car door. "I gave her a good test drive. Everything's checked out but let me know if you have any issues."

"I will." Excluding ditch detours, the car had never given her any problems.

It was almost a shame. Gave her no excuse to see him again.

She stepped past him and slid down behind the wheel. She adjusted the seat while he opened the bay door.

The snow had stopped falling sometime during the night, leaving snowdrifts at nearly every turn. The parking lot of Rasmussen Automotive, though, was plowed clean, all the snow mounded in a huge pile off to one side.

Mac leaned down to look in her open window. "Drive careful," he warned. "Wouldn't want another close encounter of the snow kind."

She smiled slightly. "I will. Have a very long

way to go to get to Gold Creek. Being right across the street and all." She fastened her safety belt and started the engine. "We'll be opening soon. You should come over and check it out sometime." She hadn't felt this edgy in…well…ever. "Not that you need it." She yanked her gaze away from the perfection outlined by stretchy cotton. "A workout, I mean." She felt like an idiot and shoved the car in gear.

"Easy there," he chided. "A car like her wants a confident hand. Not a rough one."

"Smart girl." Before she could embarrass herself even more, she rolled up her window and he stepped out of the way.

She sketched a quick wave and backed out of the garage. She wheeled around the big snow pile and stopped at the curb, waiting for a chance to buzz across the street, then made the mistake of looking in her rearview mirror as she left.

Mac was standing in the wide bay, arms folded across his wide chest as he watched her.

She exhaled, flexed her fingers around the steering wheel and, when the first break in traffic appeared, gunned it across the road.

When she was across, she glanced in her rearview mirror again. He was gone.

Unlike Vivian's library project, the Gold Creek Recreation Center had not been built from the ground up. At least, not all of it. The core of it had once been an abandoned commercial property. As was Vivian's habit, she'd decided the original building wasn't large enough and had expanded it. Now, the exterior work was almost complete with no hint of the original building at all. Most of the remaining renovations that had to be done were to the interior.

A fortunate thing for Delia, since that meant Nick visited the premises only occasionally to check on the progress of the construction workers.

She drove around the wings of the building and parked in the rear next to Stewart's car. She punched in the security code on the door and went inside.

The recreation center was more than just a gym. More than a place to lift weights or swim laps. It would provide a location for community classes. For camps. Preschool and after-school care. There would be something for everyone regardless of age.

It wasn't as if the idea was novel to have such services available, even in a town like Weaver. But it was new for Weaver to have everything centralized in one place, and to rid the town of an old, abandoned property in the process.

The smell of fresh paint was strong as she worked her way around painters and scaffolding to the lobby and the window-walled gymnasium where Stewart had suggested they hold the interviews for a new manager. The lobby overlooked the gym, which was by far the most finished space in the entire building.

And it had doors to close against the noise of the tradesmen's hammers and radios.

Mac's garage was perfectly visible through the windows.

"All the résumés are in the folder," Stewart said.

She turned her back on the view across the street.

Stewart was arranging chairs at a long table—two on one side and one on the other.

She flipped open the file. "Just this afternoon?" She thumbed the pages, counting quickly. "I know Vivian insists we see everyone in person who submits an application, but do we need to do it all in one day?"

He took the folder and positioned it on the table precisely between the two chairs. "I've read through them. Ten minutes per applicant is going to be more than sufficient. Only two looked the least bit promising."

She wondered what he would think of *her* résumé. If she had actually ever prepared one.

Ten minutes would be more than sufficient for her, too.

She pulled off her coat and tossed it on the end of the table. "Doesn't this, uh," she waved her hand at the arrangement, "seem sort of intimidating? You know. Us on one side of the table. Applicant on the other?"

He glanced from her coat to the door where a coatrack was located. His coat, naturally, hung perfectly from one of the hangers. "What else would you suggest?"

"Can't we just be more casual about it?" She lifted her arms, encompassing the room. Basketball nets were suspended on special devices that could be raised and lowered from the ceiling rafters. The glossy wood floor that had already been painted for a variety of court sports was covered in sheeting to protect it from the massive amounts of construction dust that was everywhere. "We're not sitting in some corporate office here. Do we really need to have a table between the chairs?"

She wondered if he was even aware of his habit of running his palm down the front of his tie. "I suppose not." He glanced at his wristwatch and adjusted his cuffs. "The first applicant is due in ten minutes."

She had to bite the inside of her cheek. "Pretty sure we can rearrange three chairs in time." She picked up her puffy pink coat. "With time to spare for me to hang this up." She carried it over to the coatrack and slid it onto a hanger. It looked outclassed in every way by his black wool overcoat.

Then she grouped the three chairs together and away from the table. "Now it feels more like we're just having a conversation," she said.

"If someone feels intimidated during an interview, they're probably not the best choice for a managerial position." He picked up the folder and handed it to her. "But you're the boss."

"Not by choice," she muttered. And she'd never had a job interview when she *hadn't* felt both intimidated and wildly unqualified.

She sat down in one of the chairs and crossed her legs. Unlike Stewart, she was not wearing a suit. Not that she didn't own one. She just usually saved it for funerals.

Instead, she wore skinny jeans tucked into boots Grace had given her and a sequined sweater.

She flipped open the folder and pretended to study the first page.

He sat down and pulled out his cell phone. "I hope the mechanic didn't overcharge you."

"I'm sure he didn't." She flipped to the second page and pretended to study it as well. *How* could she have ever entertained the idea that Stewart was attractive?

"They get away with a lot. Because so many customers don't know any different."

"Sort of like lawyers," she said, and gave him a sweet smile.

The remaining six minutes felt like sixty and she was eternally grateful when the first applicant was a few minutes early.

After they'd met with the five that followed, Delia had to reluctantly admit that Stewart had been right about the ten-minute time slots.

None of the people who showed up during that first hour were at all right for the job. Even Delia could tell that.

Too inexperienced. Too much experience. One could only work part-time. One could work full-time but only if his probation officer agreed. One came in who *seemed* qualified but was moving out of the state in two months, and one didn't show up at all.

Delia wandered through the building to kill some time while they waited for the seventh applicant. A small crew was working on the swimming pool, installing tile. She watched them for a moment. There wasn't a single indoor swimming pool in the entire region.

Trust Vivian to take care of that.

She returned to the gymnasium to see a truck parked in the front parking lot. Across the street, she could see three cars sitting in the bays.

She took her seat again. Stewart didn't look up from his cell phone as he handed her the folder again.

She took it but didn't bother looking inside. Stewart had been doing all the talking anyway. She stifled a yawn and watched a car pull into Mac's parking lot. Just six more people to see.

And then what?

If none of them worked out, how many more applicants could they expect to come out of the woodwork?

"Hi, I'm here about—"

She looked around when the woman spoke.

Charmaine Macdonald stood in the doorway to the gym, looking just as surprised as Delia felt. "About the manager position?"

Stewart had popped out of his chair and Delia stood, too. "Charmaine. Hi." She gestured at the third chair. "Come on in. Have a seat. This is, ah, Stewart St. James," she introduced.

The bartender's smile was a little stiff, but she swiftly crossed the room, her hand extended. She wasn't in a suit exactly, but her navy blazer and blue jeans hit closer to the mark than Delia's attire. "Mr. St. James. Nice to meet you."

"Mr. St. James is my father." He smiled winningly. "Call me Stewart."

Feeling invisible again, Delia sat when they sat. She glanced inside the folder, quickly scanning the résumé. If she'd been thorough enough to read the names in the first place, she'd have been prepared.

Charmaine folded her coat on her lap and looked from Stewart to Delia and back again. "I appreciate your time," she began. "I pass by here every day. It's been quite something to see the transformation."

Delia closed the folder and clasped her hands on top of it. "Why do you want to leave Colbys?" As an interview question, it undoubtedly left a lot to be desired, but she didn't care.

Instead of her usual braids, Charmaine's brilliant red hair was loose. She tucked it behind her ear. "Colbys has been a great place to work. I can't say enough good things about the ownership."

"But…?" There was always a but.

"I have two teenagers at home who need a parent around who doesn't work until midnight."

"What about the hours here? What if there are days when you can't leave the second you have to pick up one of them from school?"

"They both walk home from school," Charmaine answered smoothly. "And I've read about the after-school activities that're going to be held here. I intend signing them up whether I'm employed here or not. The only days they aren't free is Tuesdays. As for management experience, I've been with Colbys for five years and for the last two have handled most of the managerial duties on top of bartending."

"Why not Tuesdays?" She ignored the look she earned from Stewart.

Charmaine didn't seem to notice it at all, probably because she was fumbling with her coat. "They spend Tuesday afternoons with Mac." She pulled out a long envelope. "Here are a couple letters of recommendation. One is from Janie Clay. I didn't have time to email—"

"That's fine," Stewart assured her, taking the envelope and handing it off to Delia. "According to your résumé, you've also worked in retail?"

"At Classic Charms here in Weaver for three years, plus Shop-World for a few months. It was just a holiday stint but that was enough for me to realize I prefer working for local companies over large corporations. And before that, I had a job in Braden managing the movie theater—I know it's closed now but this was a good ten years ago. It was just the drive back and forth got to be a bit much. There are too many accidents on that highway, you know?"

Delia had been born and raised in Braden. She'd spent a lot of time at the movie theater. She didn't remember ever seeing Charmaine there. She did agree though about the highway. The thirty-mile stretch between Weaver and Braden was narrow and winding and easily congested as a result. She'd probably driven back and forth on it a thousand times. "Do you have references?"

"Several," Stewart answered before Charmaine could. "They're listed on her résumé."

Delia's smile felt tight. His message was clear. She should have reviewed the paperwork better. "We also require a background check of all employees." She'd heard him say that often enough over the last hour, too.

"Which we will arrange, naturally, when the time comes," Stewart finished. "Delia, why don't you take the next appointment while I give Charmaine a tour?"

Not that he waited around for her agreement before ushering Charmaine out of the gymnasium.

She sighed and slid her fingernail beneath the envelope flap to pull out Charmaine's letters of recommendation.

They were both typed with handwritten signatures. The first one was full of accolades and signed by Jane Clay. The second one was almost terse in comparison. Just a few sentences attesting to Charmaine's reliability and fine character. It was signed by Mac Jeffries. *Proprietor* of Rasmussen Automotive.

Why had he let her think he was only an employee there?

Just having a little laugh at her expense?

Or equally likely, he didn't give two figs what she thought. After all, he spent every Tuesday afternoon with Charmaine Macdonald's kids…

She folded the letters, tucked them back inside the envelope and stuck it inside the folder. She paged through the rest of the résumés, reading them quickly but thoroughly even though she already knew it would be pointless.

Stewart had said at the outset that they had only two real possibilities. The first one they'd already seen but she was moving away soon. The second was obviously Charmaine.

With Delia using an office at Gold Creek for her foundation work, she'd be seeing the woman regularly.

Maybe Charmaine and Mac are just friends.

Delia grimaced.

Her luck was never that good.

The rest of the interviews went about as Delia had expected. Which was to say that Charmaine's qualifications were even more pronounced in comparison to the rest—who had none.

She would have liked to leave the task of offering Charmaine the job to Stewart. But it smacked of cowardice. When she told him she would make the offer herself, he didn't look displeased. Just surprised. Then he made her write down a list of dos and don'ts to keep in mind.

So after they'd done the video call with the web designer and Stewart headed off to take care of his own matters, Delia phoned Charmaine. First at home, where she got only the answering machine.

Not even her kids were there. It was Tuesday. No doubt they were with Mac.

His garage doors had closed again while she and Stewart had been hunched around his laptop for the video call.

Ignoring the pinching pain behind her forehead, Delia drove to Colbys. The streets were fully cleared now, and Charmaine was, indeed, working behind the bar.

And there was no denying the quick flare of hope in the other woman's eyes when Delia stopped in front of her. "Is there somewhere we can talk for a few minutes?"

Charmaine nodded and called one of the servers over before leading the way to a small, cramped office. "If you're here to tell me you've found someone more suitable—"

Apparently, Delia *wasn't* the only one to suffer crises of confidence. "The job's yours," she interrupted. "If you want it."

Charmaine stared unblinkingly for an uncomfortable length of time. "Really," she finally said. "You're serious?"

"The sooner you can start, the better. The grand opening is already scheduled for Valentine's Day, and you saw for yourself the amount of work still needed before the center's ready."

"What about the background thing?"

"We'll have to take care of it along the way. You won't be working directly with kids to start with anyway. For now, we need to get the place ready to open. It's not a problem, is it?"

"No. No, of course not." Charmaine's hair was back in braids again and she flipped them behind her shoulder. "Obviously, I want the job, but the salary—"

Delia named a sum.

Charmaine's eyebrows rose slightly. "That's not quite as much as I'd hoped," she said bluntly. "The range in the advertisement went higher. I make more than that here at the bar."

Delia had no idea that bartending was so lucrative. "It's exactly what Marty Wells was being paid. But you and your family will have full access to the rec center at no cost. So those after-school activities you're interested in will be a full perk." The cost wasn't prohibitive to begin with, but it was still an incentive. "Then there's the benefit package. Medical, dental, vision. Life."

Charmaine rubbed the back of her neck, seeming torn. "I need to think about it. Can I give you an answer in a day or two?"

Delia nodded. "I'm sure Stewart told you earlier that we've been advertising for the rest of the staff that Marty didn't get to before he left. If you do take the job, then obviously getting the rest of the positions filled will be one of your top priorities. Plus dealing with the construction crews and the preregistrations that have been coming in for the last month. The next few weeks will be incredibly busy—"

"—are you trying to talk me out of it?"

Was she? Delia shook her head, hoping it wasn't a lie. She'd never had a problem with Charmaine before. Which meant if she did now, it was only because of the other woman's apparent involvement with Mac. A man who had *no* involvement with Delia.

She wasn't really that shallow, was she?

"No. I hope you *do* take the job." Okay, that was premature, but she could will herself into that positive frame of mind. "But if you do take it, I don't want you to feel like you've been tossed in over your head."

Unlike the way she'd felt every single day since Vivian's New Year's Day announcement.

Charmaine looked thoughtful. "Fair enough." She led the way back into the bar. "I'll let you know one way or the other soon. Should I call you? Or Stewart? I wasn't really clear on who's in charge."

Delia smiled, though there was no humor in it. "That would be me," she admitted. And probably time she acted like it. "Stewart's here only temporarily."

"Not surprised. That suit of his? Doesn't exactly fit in around here." Charmaine picked up two empty beer bottles on her way behind the bar once more. "Pity though."

"Why?"

"He's a good-looking suit."

Delia thought about Mac. His suit had been a pair of coveralls that zipped over a plain T-shirt and jeans.

She turned down Charmaine's offer of a hot drink and left. She drove past the sheriff's department and the town square. Past the Finley Memorial Library. Maybe she was just a glutton for punishment, she realized, when she drove past Nick's office.

His truck sat in the parking lot.

Annoyed with herself, she turned around at the next corner and headed back. Mac's garage was almost on the edge of town. She couldn't help slowing as she passed it, too.

There were several cars there now and one of the bays was open.

All she could see inside it, though, was an old truck with its hood up.

The old Delia would have stopped. She'd have made up some excuse that her car was making a funny noise even if it weren't. She'd have smiled and flirted and left again, never taking any of it seriously.

The vehicle behind her tooted its horn.

She sighed faintly and sped up again.

Some days, she missed the old Delia. She'd never actually cared about anything.

And she'd never been lonely.

Chapter Nine

Delia was in her car delivering Vivian's soiree invitations two days later when Charmaine called to let her know she was accepting the job offer.

Stewart had coached Delia in preparation. For her part, she'd made an honest effort to pay closer attention.

"Great. When can you start?"

"Janie's actually the one who encouraged me to apply for the job. She told me not to worry about serving notice, but I don't want to leave her in a total lurch. So I thought Monday would be fair."

It left only a week until the rec center's grand opening, but Delia wasn't going to quibble about it. "I have an onboarding package put together that you'll need to complete before you start work." In anticipation of the hiring blitz, she'd made up several packets. They were sitting on the passenger seat beside her, along with Vivian's invitations. "I'm heading to Braden right now, but I can drop it off to you later. Colbys or your home—"

"Colbys would be great if you really don't mind. I'm off at six, though. There's a school thing tonight. I can always run by and pick it up if we miss each other."

"Colbys it is, then."

"Thanks, Delia. I'm really looking forward to the opportunity."

She sounded it, too.

The call ended and Delia's radio took over the speakers once more.

Driving into the town of Braden felt as comfortable as a pair of old boots. She headed straight to her parents' house first. She knew her dad would be at the office and wasn't certain that her mom would be home at all, but when she entered the house, her mom was descending the stairs with a basket of laundry in her arms.

"Honey! Why didn't you tell me you were stopping by?" Season Templeton was as blonde as Delia was dark. She quickly skipped down the rest of the stairs, dropped the basket on the floor and wrapped her arms around Delia in a big rocking hug as if it had been four years rather than four weeks since they'd last seen each other. Her mom pushed her back to peer into her face. "How is all of this foundation business going with Vivian?"

"It's going," she said wryly. "That's about all I can say at this point."

"Your dad has been nearly worrying himself sick about it. He doesn't want Vivian disappointing you."

"She's not going to disappoint me."

"You've known her a handful of years. He doesn't find it so easy to accept that she's changed that much since he was young." Season stooped to pick up her basket and propped it on her slender hip. "You're looking too thin. Is Montrose causing you grief? Have you had lunch yet? Tell me what's on your mind."

Delia couldn't help smiling a little. Before she'd been born, her mother had been a practicing psychologist. Delia had figured that was the reason why her mom was always so full of questions. It was only as she got older and all the friends around her were having families of their own that she realized questions about their kids' lives consumed most mothers.

"I'm no thinner today than I was six months ago," Delia said. "Montrose is the same as always, and I *was* hoping I could grab something to eat. That's why I stopped here first before going by Uncle Carter and Aunt Meredith's." Much as she loved her quirky aunt, there was *no* comparison between Season's cooking skills and her sister-in-law's. Meredith was sure to offer food. But she was always experimenting with one cooking fad or another and the results were often less than edible.

"Come on then." Her mother led the way into the kitchen where she nudged aside several children's books to set the laundry basket on the counter. "I made soup and sourdough just yesterday." She was a whirr of motion, opening the refrigerator and starting a flame under the pot she set on the stove. "Not that you ever need a reason to come home, but what—"

Delia held up the parchment envelope with her parents' names written on the front. "From Vivian. She's having a *soiree*."

"Well, that'll thrill your father." Her mother plucked the envelope from her fingers and quickly read the message inside. "I hope she's not planning to drop any more little bombshells like she did on New Year's." She fastened the handwritten invitation to the refrigerator with a magnet bearing Delia's two-year-old nephew's face.

"You mean putting me in charge of the foundation?"

Her mother just gave her a look that had Delia feeling as small as the magnet.

"I was talking about her and Squire finally burying the hatchet, actually." Season filled two bowls with steaming vegetable soup and set them on the table. Delia washed her hands at the sink and pulled out spoons. When she sat down at the table, her mom had added a cutting board with a sourdough round that would have made Montrose proud.

"They *say* they've buried the hatchet." Delia cut a slice of bread and inhaled the aroma. "But so far they can't even agree on a real name for the foundation, much less the types of activities they want to fund. It's a good thing the website people are in California and all our meetings have been on the computer. They'd probably tell us to take a hike otherwise."

"Why'd you hire someone out in California?"

"Stewart recommended them." She picked up her spoon and dipped it into the chunky soup. Her mom had always made the best soups.

"And how *are* things going with Stewart?"

Delia lifted a shoulder. "Fine. He's got a lot of advice, that's for sure."

"Most lawyers do," Season said. Wryly, considering they had several lawyers in the family.

Delia studied the chunk of carrot on her spoon. "I think Vivian is attempting a little matchmaking."

"This is a surprise? Are you saying you didn't have even a little bit of interest in Stewart at the beginning?"

She grimaced. "Trust me, it didn't last."

Happy New Year.

She focused harder on the soup. Banishing Mac from her mind was proving difficult. "Vivian would do better to look for number five for herself than worry about my love life."

When Delia arrived at her aunt and uncle's house after she'd finished lunch with her mom, Meredith expressed similar surprise over Squire and Vivian as she tacked Vivian's invitation on a flowered bulletin board in her kitchen. "I wonder what Squire's wife makes of it."

"I heard Gloria's spending the winter in Arizona. Maybe she doesn't even know. Or care."

Meredith dismissed the idea with a *pfft*. She set a

dark, seemingly perfect brownie on a napkin in front of Delia. "Of course she knows. And she's not in Arizona. She's back and staying at her daughter's place."

"Think she and Squire will get back together?"

"They've been married a long time. Seems a terrible shame if they don't. I heard the whole reason she walked out on him was because she got fed up with his attitude toward Vivian." She nudged the napkin. "You're too thin."

"No, I'm not." But Delia dutifully took a bite of the brownie. It tasted like chalk.

"What do you think?" Meredith beamed. "I'm experimenting with roasting my own cocoa beans."

All Delia could do was smile and nod wordlessly. She was too busy trying not to choke.

After Meredith, she dropped off envelopes at her brother's house—where her cousin Archer happened to conveniently be visiting—before quickly making the rounds to the rest of her cousins' homes. Fortunately, her need to get back to Weaver was more than an excuse, so she couldn't linger for long, thus avoiding more questions about their grandmother and her inexplicable partnership with Squire.

Her last stop on the way back to Weaver was Ali and Grant's place. She didn't care whether they were home or not; she intended to drop the invitation and run.

Ali was a cop. When she started with the questions, she was merciless, and Delia had always found her husband, Grant—a successful thriller writer—unnervingly intense.

She parked in front of their house, silently hurried up the front porch, cracked open the storm door enough to slide the envelope through, and snuck away.

She was gleefully escaping unscathed down the long, private drive from their house toward the highway when she saw flashing blue and red lights in her rearview mirror.

She swore under her breath and slowed to a stop while Ali's police-issued SUV came abreast.

Delia rolled down her window and glared at her cousin. "Don't pretend this is an official stop," she warned as Ali got out of the car and approached.

Her cousin's eyes were merry when she tipped down her mirrored aviator-style sunglasses. She leaned her forearms on Delia's opened window and her dark brown canvas coat crinkled. "Not sure what the code would be for hit and run with a Vivian-invite."

"I figured you'd be on duty this time of day."

Ali patted her seriously expanded belly. "Reduced hours as the countdown begins."

After so many of her cousins having babies lately, Delia no longer bothered trying to squelch her spurts of envy. "Admit it. You're grabbing some hot afternoon delight with your husband while you can before your next field goal kicker arrives."

Ali laughed. "If only. Said husband is out with a friend on an errand. He should be back soon though, while I've got to pick up our first kicker from daycare in a bit. So who all is Viv summoning this time?"

"The usual suspects."

"Anyone on Squire's side?"

She shook her head.

"Anyone who isn't family?"

She shook her head again. "Well, except for Stewart St. James," she qualified. "Vivvie can't very well exclude him when he's staying in the guesthouse."

Ali's eyes sharpened even more. "I've heard your pal Stewie is pretty easy on the eyes. Anything interesting going on there?"

"Does everyone think my only hope of finding a man is if Vivian arranges it?"

Ali's grin didn't dim one watt. "You've gotta admit, you've kind of run through most of the available stock."

"Just because I used to date a lot of guys didn't mean I was sleeping my way through them." Frankly, the birth control implant in her arm had been going to waste for nearly three years now.

Ali winked. "Just a few of them. Shoot, Delia." She straightened and pressed her hands to her back as she arched. "I used to be jealous as all get-out when it comes to your ability to charm every male in your vicinity."

She turned up her heater to combat having her window down. "Yeah, well, I guess I lost the knack where Nick was concerned."

"Please. Nick wasn't right for you, and we all knew it. He's too…too…"

Delia's lips twisted. "Nice for the likes of me?"

"I was thinking of tame. But he *is* nice." Ali

winked. "Even for the likes of you." Her attention perked for a moment at the pickup truck heading their way. "There's Grant. *You*," she didn't miss a beat, "just fixated on Nick 'cause he was conveniently there working with Vivian all the time. While all around you, we were dropping like flies into marital bliss, leaving you the old maid."

Delia made a face. "Trust you to make me feel *so* much better."

Ali laughed. "That's why you've always loved me best."

Annoyingly, it was sort of true. Ali's bubble was a little off center among her set of siblings just as Delia's was among hers.

"Seriously, though. I say let go and live on, you know? Not once did I ever see you look at Nick with your heart in your eyes. Half the reason guys fall over themselves where you're concerned are those big ol' Bambi eyes you've got going on. Well, that and your boobs."

"Give me a break," Delia muttered.

But Ali wasn't paying any attention because the pickup truck had stopped in front of the SUV, and she was bounding—much too energetically for someone who was as pregnant as she was—over to it.

Delia really needed to get going so she didn't get caught in what passed for rush hour between Braden and Weaver. She let her car roll forward until her window was even with Grant's. She could see he had a passenger with him.

She stuck her head out her window, intending to

wave an expedient hello-and-goodbye before getting on down the road. "Yo, Grant! Don't think you and Ali are going to get out of Vivian's next party by having that baby. I told Hayley and Seth the same thing when I dropped off their invite." Ali's older sister was as near to popping as Ali was. Seth, with his mile-wide protective streak, was even taking time off work already to make sure Hayley didn't overdo it.

Grant was sending his wife a wary look. "*Another* party?"

"Friday after next," Ali said, stepping up onto the running board to give him a kiss through the window."

"And I know how all of you like to work the system," Delia warned, "so I'm going to want proof of contractions if any one of you tries using labor as an excuse to miss it."

"All I know is that Hayley is *not* going to beat us to the delivery room," Ali said fervently. "And I just realized I'm being totally rude." She pivoted so she was no longer blocking the truck's window. "My cousin, Delia. Delia, this is Grant's friend." As she spoke, Grant leaned back, and his friend in the seat next to him leaned forward. "Mac Jeffries," Ali introduced. "He owns that automotive place in Weaver out on Twelfth where the highway turns into Main—"

All Delia could do was stare.

"We've met." Below the brim of his cowboy hat, Mac's blue gaze seemed to capture hers. "Car's running okay for you?"

"Um. Yeah. Like a top." She finally managed to look away, only to trip into the speculation on Ali's face. She quickly focused on Grant, who suddenly seemed the safest port. "How, uh, how do you know each other?"

"Grant's gotten caught up in one of Mac's side gigs," Ali answered before he could.

"I'm not caught up," Grant said.

"It's not a side gig," Mac said.

None of which explained anything at all to Delia. "Well, cool," she said just for something to say. "And I've really got to go." She tapped the stack of employment packages she'd made. "We hired a manager to replace Marty Wells at the rec center." She felt odd not identifying that person as Charmaine. But she was sure the woman would convey that information to Mac on her own. "Need to take care of the paperwork."

Ali was still hanging on the side of the pickup truck. "Just watch yourself on the highway," she warned. "You never see black ice until it's too late."

Delia was used to these cautionary nuggets. Since Ali routinely dealt with accidents in the course of her job, Delia supposed her cousin had earned the right.

"I'm always careful." Her gaze skated over Mac, and feeling flushed, she pressed the gas pedal.

It was her own damned luck that the back end of her car fishtailed before she'd even gotten out of their sight. She let off the gas and turned into the skid until she had it under control again.

Chapter Ten

It figured that Delia ended up getting stuck behind a pickup truck hauling a trailer of livestock on the winding road back to Weaver and it took twice as long as usual for her to reach the outskirts of town.

The streetlights were coming on as she slowed down again to creep through town. A couple years ago the traffic had been a fraction of what it was now. She blamed most of it on the new state park, but Gage's resort up on the mountain shared some of the blame. The inaugural ski season at Angel's Flight was supposedly beating all expectations.

According to Vivian, Gage and his wife had been staying up at the resort for the last few days. But Delia had no desire to spend more time in her car, driving up there to deliver his invitation.

And she definitely had no desire to see the resort itself. Maybe it was illogical, but if Gage hadn't hired Megan to design the equestrian center at Angel's Flight, she and Nick would have probably never met.

Not that Delia would be any less alone now.

A long line of brake lights stretched out ahead of her, and she abruptly turned down a side street to avoid it all. She wound her way through one neighborhood after another and eventually came out at the edge of town.

Right next to the Rasmussen Automotive sign.

How many times had she driven by without giving it any notice at all?

She rested her arms on top of her steering wheel, looking from the rec center to the garage across the street. Once again, all the bay doors were closed. But a light shined through the windows of the office where a *closed* sign was lit in red.

Her phone rang, sounding loud through her car speakers. She glanced at her phone display and thumbed the button on her steering wheel. "What's up, Stewart?"

"Just got a copy of the occupancy inspection from Nick Ventura. Gold Creek's good to go."

"That's great news. Thanks."

"I'm scheduling another video appointment with the website designer for tomorrow. What time works best for you?"

She took a last look at Mac's garage. "Any time is fine." She turned back onto Main Street. At least she was out of the worst of the traffic now as she headed back into the center of town. "I don't know what we're going to talk about though."

"There's still plenty of content for us to put together. But I asked my father to give Vivian a call. See if he can nudge her along to resolve things more with Squire."

She supposed it was worth a shot. Stewart's father was Vivian's oldest and most trusted advisor.

"I'll be in touch about the meeting. Meanwhile, have you finished reading those articles I gave you?"

"Just about," she said brightly. An utter lie.

Fortunately, Stewart had another call coming in. He hung up and Delia didn't have to elaborate.

Even from a distance, she could see the parking lot at Colbys was full as usual.

She parked in front of Classic Charms and stopped long enough to glance in the display window. The eclectic boutique was her favorite place to shop, offering everything from the occasional piece of furniture to sexy lingerie to wedding gowns. Today, the window was filled with a family of bears dressed in heart-patterned sweaters.

She didn't need the reminder that Valentine's Day was growing near, considering all of the work still yet to be done at Gold Creek before they opened.

She felt the wind at her back as she walked the rest of the way to Colbys. It nearly yanked the door out of her hand when she pulled it open, and she swore when the manila envelope containing Charmaine's forms slid out of her grasp and went skittering across the sidewalk.

She chased after it, only to slip on an icy patch and bang into the hood of a parked truck.

The vehicle stopped her progress, but her envelope just kept sliding. Right between the tires and out of sight.

She swore all over again and went down on her hands and knees, trying to reach it.

"Having a little trouble there?"

She slowly sat back on her heels and looked at the truck ten inches away from her nose.

What was that saying?

Sometimes you were the windshield. Sometimes you were the bug.

"Hey, Nick." She took the hand he extended and let him pull her to her feet. "Thanks." Ali's comments felt stingingly fresh in her mind. "What're you doing here?"

His smile was the same easy one he'd always had for Delia. Falling for another woman hadn't changed that at all. "More to the point, what're *you* doing?"

She gestured at the ground. At least his wife wasn't with him. She didn't have to suffer Megan seeing her crawl around on the dang ground. Particularly when it occurred to her that she could have just left the packet where it was and gotten another from her car. "Lost an envelope under there," she admitted. "Couldn't reach it."

"Easy enough to solve." He got inside the truck, started the engine and backed up a few feet.

She gave a thumbs-up, snatched the envelope off the street and returned to the sidewalk.

He parked once more and joined her. "Doesn't look too much the worse for wear." He dashed his fingers across a clump of snow clinging to the envelope.

"I'm sure it's fine." She swiped it down the side of her coat for good measure and turned toward Colbys.

He fell into step with her. "Looks like we're heading to the same place."

"Looks like." She wanted to gnash her teeth. "I won't be staying long, though."

"Wish I could say the same." He looked rueful. "Have another meeting with a new client but I'd rather be home. Can't even describe what it's like to know Robin's at home starting to smile but I'm here talking to a guy about a barn conversion." He reached for the door, oblivious to the wind that was still blowing.

"Sounds like parenthood suits you." Gnashing inside but blithe on the outside. That was something at least.

She ducked around him and headed through the doorway.

"Nothing like it in the world." As soon as he followed her inside, someone hailed him, and he raised his hand in acknowledgment. "Once you have kids of your own, you'll feel the same way."

If she ever had kids of her own. That day was seeming further and further away. "I'm glad for you, Nick."

He looked at her for a fraction too long. The pause

seemed to encompass their entire non-history. "Are you?"

"Yes." They weren't merely polite words. "And the sooner you deal with your client there, the sooner you can get home to your family." She gave Nick's arm a quick squeeze before heading toward the bar where Olivia was tending the beer taps.

"Hey, Delia," Olivia greeted. "How do I get in line for the money I hear you're giving away?"

Let go. Live on.

Delia smiled wryly. "Visit the *WEAVERFUNDS* website," she said. "But we're not giving away any money yet, and unless you've got a good reason for needing it, you can save yourself wasting time in line." She leaned her forearms on the bar. "Has Charmaine already left?"

"About fifteen minutes ago." Olivia set an overflowing mug on a tray and swiped her hands on the apron around her waist. "Something I can help you with?"

She handed over the envelope. It didn't look too bedraggled. "I told her I'd leave this for her."

Olivia tucked the envelope below the bar. "I'll make sure she gets it. Want a drink?"

In the mirror on the wall behind Olivia, Delia could see the reflection of a nerdy looking guy sitting at a high-top with Nick.

"Something mild." Delia looked back at Olivia. "How about Irish coffee. But go light on the Irish."

"That's almost criminal, but whatever you want." Olivia pulled down a footed glass mug.

"Mind if I order something from the grill?" Her mother's soup and sourdough felt like a long time ago. Plus, if she ate here at Colbys, she would avoid both Montrose and Stewart when she headed back to the mansion.

And Vivian couldn't make any suggestions that were clearly meant to throw Stewart and Delia together even more.

Win. Win. Win.

Olivia extended a laminated menu. "That spot at the end of the bar is free if you want it. Just move that guy's stuff off the stool. He's alone."

"Thanks." Delia headed to the end of the bar. "Mind if I sit here?"

His gaze swept her appreciatively from head to toe. "Not anymore." The coat got dumped on the floor near his pointed cowboy boots and the hat went back on his head. He wore an enormous rodeo buckle and looked like he was barely old enough to drink.

Delia couldn't help but smile. She pulled off her own coat and after draping it over the bar stool, sat on top of it. Her wallet was in the pocket and sitting on her coat was a good way of ensuring it stayed there. A good ol' trick from days gone by. "What's your name, cowboy?"

"Roddy Decker." He gave her a wide grin. "What's yours?"

Even sounded like a rodeo name. "Delia." She smiled her thanks at Olivia when she set the hot coffee drink in front of her. "You from around here, Roddy?"

His skinny chest puffed up. "Jackson. Came all the way to check out the sights on Rambling Mountain. Didn't expect they'd be better right here in this bar."

He was as innocuous as a puppy, and she lifted her mug in a toast. "You keep thinking that, Roddy." She took a cautious sip of the hot, cream-topped coffee.

Per Delia's request, Olivia had been light with the whiskey. All in all, Delia had to agree that it was nearly criminal.

She continued listening with half an ear to Roddy's cocky chatter beside her while she read through the menu. It had been a while since she'd ordered a real meal there and she was a little impressed at the new variety. Even Colbys was keeping up with the Joneses. Fortunately, though, a few items had remained sacred. When Olivia came back to check on her, she ordered one of them. A steak—medium rare—with shoestring fries.

Olivia moved away again, and Delia glanced at Roddy.

He was still going on about his PRCA rankings.

His enthusiasm for her, though, was patently obvious.

A couple of weeks ago, he'd have come in real handy.

She smiled to herself, thinking about her family's reaction if she had walked into Vivian's New Year's brunch with a kid who looked like he was half her age.

"You know," Roddy tipped his hat back and leaned

closer to her, "I got me a suite up at Angel's Flight."
He waited, his eyebrows practically waggling.

She just laughed. "Good for you, Roddy. But offers like that are *so* far in my past."

"Aww. You don't mean it." He leaned even closer
and dropped his arm boldly around her shoulder.
"The suite is real fine. Finer than anything you've
probably ever seen."

Delia laughed yet again. "I kind of doubt that."
She shrugged off his arm and took another drink.

Mac suddenly appeared, sliding between them
just in time to block Roddy's arm from trying again.

He leaned his elbow on the bar and smiled at her.
"Hey, honey."

Chapter Eleven

Hey, honey?

By some miracle, Delia didn't choke on her Irish coffee.

It was immediately apparent that Mac thought he was rescuing her. From a guy as harmless to her as a puppy.

She didn't know if she was tickled or unnerved.

Or both.

Regardless, she seemed powerless to stop her goofy smile from growing. "What took you so long?"

"Was picking up the kids." His smile was earnest, but his eyes were full of mischief. "They're in the car arguing over who has to sit in the middle seat." He glanced over his shoulder at Roddy whose consternated expression was growing. "Three of 'em," he confided. "Not counting little Duke and Molly. They're the babies."

When Mac looked back at her, the wicked glint in his eyes had grown. "Hope you're not drinking, babe. Not when you're still nursing."

Roddy shoved a wad of bills onto the bar and escaped, yanking on his coat as he bolted out the door.

Mac took his vacated seat and pushed the money and abandoned beer aside. Then he leaned over the bar, grabbed a clean white mug from the rack and filled it with coffee from the carafe sitting on a warmer.

"Nice trick there," Delia said once he'd sat back. "Getting a guy in a crowded bar to give up his seat like that."

He tipped the sugar dispenser over the mug, dispensing a small stream of granules. "Man learns a few things in his life."

She laughed softly. "Your timing *is* sort of impeccable. Is that also a learned thing or just coincidence?"

The corner of his lips tilted. "My wisdom knows no bounds." He took a sip of coffee, grimaced slightly and added more sugar.

"Try this." She nudged her Irish coffee toward him. The cream was still a thick ivory layer on top of the mixture of sweet coffee and miserly dash of whiskey. "Since you've obviously got a sweet tooth."

"Girl's drink," he said dismissively.

She laughed silently. "Talk about letting your chauvinism hang out." She wrapped her fingers around the mug handle again. "But it's your loss." She toasted him before taking a healthy swig. "What're you doing here, anyway?"

His gaze followed the platter of sizzling steak that a waitress set in front of Delia. "Same thing as you, apparently." His head swiveled to locate Olivia at the other end of the bar. "Hey, Olivia. Order me the same thing as her from the grill, will you? Rare. And add a side salad."

She gave him a thumb's-up and he looked back at Delia's plate.

"I don't think it's polite to covet someone's shoe-string fries." She moved the plate further away from him.

"You have a mountain of them. You're not gonna eat them all."

"Really?" She plucked one thin, searingly hot French fry from the stack, broke it in half and blew on it. "You've got me all figured out like that, do you?"

"Not even close." He propped his elbows on the bar and squinted as he sipped his coffee. "Damn," he muttered, setting it back down again. "Still bitter." He waved down the bartender again. "When's the last time the coffeemaker got cleaned?"

Olivia just lifted her hands and turned back to the concoction she was blending.

He slid off the bar stool. "Save that for me, would you?" He walked around Delia and lifted the hatch to go behind the bar. He dumped out his coffee mug and then, as if he had every right to do so, proceeded to also dump out both pots of coffee on the warmers. Then he began deftly dismantling the big boxy coffee brewer that sat on the back counter.

She was surprised enough by his actions that she very nearly forgot to protect his bar stool. "Sorry," she said quickly to the bleached blonde who started to shimmy her tush up onto the stool. "The seat's taken."

The blonde pouted but didn't argue. Too bad for Roddy. Had he hung around to try his moves on her he might have had more luck impressing her with his fancy suite up at Angel's Flight.

Hoping to forestall another bar stool poacher, Delia slid off her own onto Mac's and pulled her plate in front of her. The steak knife was hardly needed because the beef was so tender. She'd decimated half the mound of shoestring fries and a quarter of her rib eye by the time Mac was finished scouring the brewer and had reassembled it. As if he'd done it a million times, he added the oversized filters, filled them with fresh grounds and stuck two clean carafes beneath the spouts.

He started it brewing again and came back around to take his seat.

She scooted back over onto her own bar stool. "Oil changes *and* coffeemakers? Real renaissance man."

His shoulder brushed against hers when he shrugged and gave her plate a sideways glance.

She laughed slightly and waved her hand in invitation. "Fine. But fries only. The steak is all mine."

"I'll give you that one." He pulled several fries from the dwindling pile and ate them. "Only beef they serve here is from the Double-C. Too damn good to share."

She gave him a quick look. "I didn't know that. How do you?"

"Boundless wisdom, remember?" His blue eyes were amused. "Squire Clay's one of my biggest customers."

Her hand collided with Mac's when they both reached for another French fry and she snatched hers back, curling her fingers in her lap. "Go ahead."

"Ladies first. Particularly when they're yours to begin with."

Something was fluttering around inside her chest again. Not just attraction. She was familiar with that.

She wasn't familiar with *this*.

She reached for her Irish coffee and wished that she hadn't requested light on the Irish. "Charmaine's off," she said abruptly.

"Parent-teacher night at the school," he said without missing a beat.

Her curiosity was a lot tougher to chew on than her French fries. "You've known each other a long time?"

"Long enough. She told me about the job she's taking at Gold Creek. She'll do good work for you."

That answered at least one question.

But she was no closer to knowing how deeply they were involved. Why did it feel so hard to just ask him?

She opened her mouth. Pushed the words to the tip of her tongue. "How, uh, how…how did you and Grant meet?" *Idiot.*

"Usual way I've met most people around here," he said. "Car repairs."

At least he didn't know she was mentally kicking herself around the block. "And you became friends."

"That unusual?" He waited a beat. "I do have a few."

"I didn't mean that. It's just he's—" She broke off.

His eyebrows rose slightly. "Famous and I'm a mechanic?"

"No! He's…well, he's just different, that's all. If it weren't for Ali, I think Grant would be happy being a recluse."

Mac's lips twitched. "Some people keep their thoughts to themselves better than others."

"Unlike me, you mean?"

"If the shoe fits, Cinderella."

She made a face at him, and his twitch grew into a full-on smile.

It made her feel a little breathless, that smile.

Ali would probably have a whole lot to say about that.

"What's the side gig she mentioned you and Grant were doing?"

He made a sound. "There's no side gig."

She pursed her lips and narrowed her eyes. "I have the feeling this is one of those he who protests too much moments."

He curled his hands together, thumbs softly drumming the bar top. "I fix things," he relented finally. "Besides cars." He pulled his hands apart and sat back, crossing his arms over his chest. "Things people are getting rid of. Appliances and stuff."

"To sell? I remember a place in Braden when I was a kid. It's closed up now, but they always had refurbished fridges and wash—"

"I don't sell anything. I just usually know people in need of," he made a sound, "of appliances and stuff."

Olivia set his salad in front of him. "Mac's the ultimate recycle, repair and relieve guy." She'd obviously overheard. "Got a whole kitchen's worth of appliances to someone I know up in Wymon. Husband walked out on her and her kids. Took everything that wasn't nailed down—even the light bulbs. Weren't for Mac, not sure what they'd have done."

"Was no big deal," he muttered. He whipped off the napkin wrapped around his utensils and stabbed his fork into the lettuce.

"Was a big deal to Simone and her kids," Olivia said. She gave Delia a quick wink and grabbed her next order off the printer.

Casey Clay came out from the office behind the bar and stopped to greet them. "Hey, Delia. How's Vivian?"

"Same as ever. You and Jane are bringing your twins to the Gold Creek opening, right? I just confirmed a bounce house this morning for the little kids."

"Think Janie's got it written on the calendar." He

tilted a glass under a beer tap. "Mac, you gonna stick around later to shoot some pool?"

"Give you another opportunity to win twenty off me?"

Casey grinned. "We could go double or nothing. I'll even spot you ten. Think about it." He closed the tap and carried his beer back around to the office.

Mac glanced at Delia. "He's a pool shark."

"I think I might have heard that somewhere." She realized she was staring at the dark blond hair curling over his forehead and attacked her steak again with needless vigor. "Casey's my cousin," she said abruptly. Proving yet again that she had no verbal self-control.

Mac's gaze slid toward her, once more amused. "Is he?"

She swallowed the bite of steak in her mouth with a shameful lack of appreciation. The twin streams from the big brewer had already dribbled to a stop and the aroma of coffee was strong.

Her need to fill the silence was embarrassing. "It's complicated."

He stabbed another piece of lettuce. "Yeah?"

Someone had been feeding quarters into the jukebox and Johnny Cash's deep voice was suddenly singing about a boy named Sue. The music was loud, and she raised her voice slightly. "Squire's first wife and my grandmother's first husband were siblings. Half siblings anyway."

"Halves. Wholes. Who cares?" He pushed up the sleeves of his thermal shirt, revealing a scar on the inside of his arm that reached all the way to his wrist. It looked too jagged to be surgical. "Sounds like you and Casey are second cousins. Not really all that complicated."

"Well, yeah, when you put it like that."

His eyes crinkled.

"I guess it seems complicated just because we'd never known anything about the family connection while we were growing up." There was no explaining her compulsion to elaborate. "Not even my dad or uncle knew about it until my grandmother dropped that news on everyone after she moved here from Pennsylvania."

"Why the big secret?"

He finally looked curious, and she realized she didn't want to cast Vivian in an unflattering light. Not just the fact that she'd tried to prevent her husband from having a relationship with his illegitimate sister, but the fact that, years later, her manipulative manner had driven off her own sons. "Family issues."

"Lot of families have 'em." His tone was matter-of-fact.

She wondered if his family did. "Anyway, Squire never told anyone about that side of his wife's family, either."

"He never connected the Templeton name with your dad? He's a pediatrician in Braden, right?"

It would be nice to know as much about Mac as he seemed to know about her. "No. I mean, yes, my dad's a pediatrician. But Squire didn't connect it."

His smile had widened again.

"Let's just say Squire does *not* get along with my grandmother," Delia said.

"Then why's he partnering with her on the new foundation? What're you calling it? *WEAVER-FUNDS?*"

"The name's just a placeholder until—" She broke off. She was tired of trying to explain it. "You and Grant could add your name to the list through the site asking for a truck to deliver those appliances," she said. "It'd be more worthwhile than some of the things people have been requesting. Not that I can get my grandmother and Squire to agree on the kinds of causes they want to help fund. They can't even agree on the time of day."

"Their argument is between them though. What about the rest of you? Doesn't look like a hardship to be related to the Clays. Or vice versa. Least that's the way it looks from the outside."

"True. And at least I never unintentionally dated someone who has turned out to be a cousin." Maybe there was more Irish in her drink than she'd thought.

He arched an eyebrow. "Was that a possibility? Wasn't your family mostly over in Braden?"

"Totally, but clearly you haven't been living in Weaver long enough to grasp the finer details of small-town living. When I was a kid, you had to stick Braden and Weaver together—" she held up her hands and pressed her palms together "—just to make up one remotely complete town. I can still remember when Shop-World was built. Talk about a big deal. High school bands played, and carnival rides came to town and everything. You'd have thought the president had come to town."

He laughed softly. "You think Weaver's small town? Visit Cradle Creek some time."

Soft or not, it was a good laugh. "Is that where you're from? Cradle Creek?" She'd never even heard of it.

"Cradle Creek, Idaho. Smallest town you'll never miss." He pushed aside the salad plate when his steak was delivered by the same waitress who'd delivered Delia's.

"Do you still have family there?"

He nodded.

"Can I get you anything else?" the waitress asked him.

"One of those coffeepots over there. Just set it right here." He tapped the gleaming wood in front of him.

She took one of the carafes from the brewer and set it on the bar top, then added a fresh ceramic mug next to it before flipping through the orders in her narrow black folder. She selected one and set the slip near Delia's drink along with a couple of wrapped candies. "Can I box that up for you?"

"Not just yet." If Delia paid the check and had her leftovers boxed, she would have no reason to linger.

And she wanted to linger. She wanted to ask him more about Cradle Creek. More about his family there. And oh, yeah. What exactly was the deal between him and Charmaine?

"Take your time." The girl slid the book back into the pocket on her apron before disappearing through the archway that connected the bar and the restaurant.

Mac filled his coffee mug, took a sip, looked satisfied and turned his attention back to his plate of food. "So where's Three-piece tonight?"

She chewed the inside of her cheek to hide a smile. "Dining with my grandmother, I'm sure."

"And *you're* here."

"Something that I'll pay for in the long run," she admitted. "Not with my grandmother or Stewart—"

"Who's only here on business."

"Exactly." She didn't miss a beat. "But Montrose'll feel compelled to needle me about it."

"Because…"

"He's protective of Vivian. Doesn't want anyone taking advantage of her. Particularly the aimless granddaughter."

Mac gave her a sidelong look. "She put you in charge of her new foundation, didn't she? Guessing that was something that she and Squire would have had to agree on."

"I suppose." She had no idea how that had even come about considering the way the decision had been dumped on her as a fait accompli.

"Then I don't get the 'aimless' bit."

Delia was still pondering that when Olivia swept by again several minutes later. "Another Irish coffee for you, Delia?"

"I'm driving, so I'd better pass." The first one had

been tasty enough—despite the coffee that Mac had judged to be terrible. She could imagine how much more delicious it would be with the fresh stuff. "I will take a glass of water when you have a chance, though."

"Coming up." Olivia plucked the slip emerging from the narrow printer next to the cash register and tucked it into an empty glass that she set with a pitcher of beer on a serving tray. Then she filled a glass with ice, squirted water into it and placed it in front of Delia before heading back to the beer taps.

Delia couldn't help but notice that Olivia hadn't asked Mac if he wanted something besides coffee. "Just coffee? Sure you don't want something else to drink, too?"

"I'm sure." He sliced off a wedge of steak and gave it an appreciative look before lifting the fork to his mouth.

He narrowed his eyes, looking nearly blissful.

Happy New Year.

Her nerves prickled and she snatched up her meal tab.

"Heading out after all?" He sliced another corner off his steak.

She could see the tables behind them in the mirror. They were nearly all occupied, but there were several bar stools now standing vacant. Saying she wanted to free up a lone bar stool at the end of the row for the restaurant's sake wouldn't wash. "I have a bunch of material Stewart expects me to read through before tomorrow."

"About?"

"Best practices for running a private foundation." At least that was what one of the articles had been titled.

"Sounds dull, but not exactly aimless."

It sounded dull to her, too. "How did you end up owning Rasmussen Automotive?"

"Earl Rasmussen was my uncle. When he died, someone needed to take it over. I got elected."

"By?"

"My mom. Earl was her brother."

"No kids of his own?"

"You mean my cousins?" His smile was teasing. "None that like getting grease under their nails ten days a week."

She glanced at his hands. His fingers were long. Slightly bony. No grease anywhere. Her gaze crept to his sinewy wrists, then his forearms again. She wondered how he'd earned the scar. It was the only point of imperfection in his sinewed forearms.

"You related to Pam and Rob Rasmussen then?"

"More distantly than you're related to the Clays."

Realizing she was still ogling his forearms she leaned over to retrieve her wallet from her zippered coat pocket, hoping to hide the fact that she'd managed to wad the check into a crumpled mess. She extracted enough cash to cover the bill plus a tip and tucked it all beneath the edge of her plate before shoving the wallet back in the pocket.

When she straightened again, she found Mac watching her. Her nerve endings tingled.

"Charmaine conveyed your New Year's Eve message, by the way."

The tingle turned into an outright jangle. Looking away from him took more willpower than she possessed. "Oh?"

"Something about soaking my head?"

She recalled a lot of swearing, too, and wondered if that had been conveyed as well. "I had too much to drink that night."

"I know."

She finally managed to pull her gaze free. It escaped as far as his jaw. The sharp line was softened slightly by stubble.

Prickly? Or soft?

Her fingers actually twitched.

She snatched up one of the small candies and unwrapped it. "I wasn't so far gone that I was incapable of getting myself home." She shoved the chocolate mint into her mouth.

He wasn't smiling. Not exactly. "I *was* tempted, you know."

She swallowed. Mint. Chocolate. Nerves. "Tempted?"

"To make it a real offer."

"Offer?" Was that all she was capable of now? Parroting words?

His eyes were so, so blue. "To take you home."

"Would have saved yourself forty dollars." *Better, Delia. An actual quip.*

"Not your home. Mine."

"I wasn't looking for...for that."

"Sure about that?"

No. "Yes." She swallowed again. "I told you. I'd had too much to drink."

"Why was that?"

The question didn't sound judgmental, yet she felt defensive anyway. "It was New Year's Eve! Everyone was drinking."

"Not everyone."

Her gaze slid to the coffeepot. His mug. "Do you ever?"

"No." He wasn't flippant like her. Nor did he sound particularly solemn. More like he was just stating a simple fact. Like the sun coming up every morning and going down every night.

"Teetotaler. I've heard of them." She stood and flicked her coat off the stool. "Sound decision. Bet it saves a ton when it comes to eating out." She pushed her arms into her coat sleeves and pulled out her keys. "Enjoy the rest of your meal." She pushed the second mint toward him. "Have an extra chocolate mint on me."

He smiled slightly and shook his head.

"Don't like chocolate?"

"Don't like mint."

"There you go." She didn't even know what she meant by that, except that some sort of response seemed required.

"Well. See you around," she said abruptly as she about-faced and headed for the door.

Brilliant.

The cold weather was a welcome slap against her

hot face, and she belatedly zipped up her coat as she hurried back down the block to her car.

She turned the key and was grateful deep down in her soul when the engine purred to life.

She realized she hadn't even noticed whether Nick was still at the restaurant.

Instead it was Mac on her mind all the way home.

Chapter Twelve

Mac studied the mammoth-sized wood door flanked by oversized sconces that lit the entire entryway.

Did he use the heavy brass door knocker?

Did he push the doorbell button?

Both?

He didn't like uncertainty. The moment he'd been old enough, he'd rid as much of it from his life as he'd been able.

It wasn't the protocol of the mansion's front door that was nagging at him like a sore tooth, though.

It was the fact that he was standing there at all.

He'd saved Delia's cell phone number on his phone. He could have just called her.

Probably should have just called her.

Why the *hell* hadn't he just called her?

Swearing under his breath, he raked his fingers through his hair and jammed his cowboy hat back in place.

He chose the brass door knocker.

The clang was still reverberating when the door swung inward to reveal Montrose.

Mac had never been to the front door—or any other door—of the mansion before. Yet Montrose didn't look surprised at all to see him there.

Must have security cameras. Or else the old guy was used to people dropping by the mansion at nine at night with no warning whatsoever.

"Mr. Jeffries." Montrose pulled the door wide and stepped out of the way. "Won't you come in." It wasn't a question but more of a command veiled in politeness.

Same attitude he always showed when he brought the Rolls into the garage.

Mac doffed his cowboy hat and stepped inside.

By some miracle, he managed not to gape. He liked thinking that he wasn't overly impressed by the trappings of wealth. He knew people who didn't have two pennies to rub together who outclassed many who did.

But just the foyer alone?

Its two stories were high and wide enough for a truck to drive through. A sea of white marble flowed across the floor. Two widespread columns were dead ahead of him.

They flanked an ornate table bearing an enormous floral arrangement that was like something out of the celebrity magazines his mom collected.

He squeezed his hat between his fingers. "I'm here to see Delia."

Montrose's nearly bald eyebrows rose slightly. "I'll inform her she has a guest."

Mac hoped that meant she was here. The only vehicle parked in the courtyard had a rental company sticker on the window. Probably what Three-piece was driving when he wasn't steering Delia's Porsche into a ditch. "Thanks."

It seemed to be what Montrose was waiting for. "I'll show you to the library." He inclined his head slightly. "You'll be more comfortable waiting there."

As opposed to what? Standing in the mausoleum-style foyer with its pot of flowers taller than Mac?

He followed Montrose past the columns and into a room lined with tall built-in bookshelves. They had a lumberyard's worth of fluted molding, and a rolling ladder provided access to the upper shelves.

There were vases, busts and whatnot interspersed among the books, which were monotone and rigidly identical in size. They reminded him of the set of overpriced encyclopedias a salesman had once talked his mom into buying. But instead of thirty volumes that had taken his mom a long time to pay off, he was looking at about twenty times that.

"May I take your coat?"

"I won't be staying long."

Montrose inclined his head once more. "Very

good." He backed out of the library, pulling the French doors closed after him.

Mac felt a full minute tick off inside his head.

Then he went over to the door and grasped the knob. It turned silently and he let go of it. All right. Good deal. *Not* locked in with the books and art that was worth who knew how much.

He tapped his hat against his thigh and went to look out the window. The evening was already dark as pitch, but the mansion had plenty of outdoor lighting.

He realized he was overlooking the huge courtyard when he recognized his own pickup off in one corner. In the other, he saw the six-door garage, as well as another smaller building he hadn't noticed earlier.

Guesthouse?

Where Montrose lived?

Why even speculate?

He was only there to give Delia back her wallet.

He'd spotted it on the floor at Colbys when he'd been paying for his supper.

He could have left it with Olivia. She'd have called Delia. Arranged to keep it safe until she could pick it up.

Instead, he'd stuffed it in his pocket and told Olivia that he would deliver it. Just in case Delia noticed and retraced her steps to find it.

Considering he'd hung out at Colbys for a few hours playing pool with Casey after she'd left, he was betting that she hadn't noticed.

He pulled off his coat and dropped it on one of the dark leather sofas arranged in a U-shape around a big square coffee table with a glass top. They faced the one wall not covered with bookshelves; it was covered with framed paintings instead.

He tossed his hat on top of his coat and moved closer to the paintings. Looking at them up close gave him no more a sense of whether they were originals or copies. But considering all the other trappings, he was guessing the former.

He stepped away from them when he heard the faint creak of the doors opening.

But it wasn't Delia who entered. It was Montrose, carrying a large gold tray.

It looked heavy and Mac automatically started to reach out to help but the cool stare he earned had him just running his hand around the back of his neck instead.

Montrose set the tray in the center of a gleaming wood table that had matching candelabras at both ends and began unloading it.

Mac eyed the fussy cups and saucers. They looked like they'd snap if a person held one too tightly. In addition to the delicate cups and the tall silver coffee server, there was also a small, tiered stand filled with a dozen tiny pastel-colored cookies.

Montrose spent a minute arranging everything, and then carried the tray back out of the room as ceremoniously as he'd entered. Before he could close the doors behind him, though, Delia arrived, pushing the doors open wide.

She stopped short at the sight of Mac. "What are *you* doing here?"

"Who were you expecting?"

"Stew—" She broke off, sending a look over her shoulder at the departing Montrose.

She dashed her fingers through her disheveled hair and gave Mac a self-conscious smile. Her feet were bare, and she was wearing red-and-white striped leggings and a matching long-sleeved T-shirt.

She looked like a candy cane topped by a swirl of dark hair and enormous hazel eyes.

"Sorry. I would have gotten dressed if Sir Loquacious had told me *you* were here." She folded her arms across her chest. "What, uh, what *are* you—" Her lips rounded silently when he held out the wallet.

"Saw it underneath the bar stool when I was leaving Colbys."

She looked chagrined. "I didn't even notice I'd dropped it. Thank you." She took a few steps closer and took it from him with extreme care.

As if she didn't want their fingers to touch.

Then she folded her arms again, wallet in hand.

Somehow, he managed to keep his gaze from the curves plumped even more by her folded arms.

"You, uh, you could have just called," she said.

"Yeah." She wasn't wearing a lick of makeup now but her wide eyes were still luminous. In her bare feet, she didn't even come up to his shoulder.

He looked away from her face to the wall of paintings. "Any fakes there?"

"What do you think?" She set her wallet next to

a dainty cup perched on a saucer. "There are a few in the collection that date back to my great-great grandfather. The most recent additions are those two skinny ones. They're by Adelaide Arians. She painted them as a special gift for Vivian."

"Never heard of her." He smiled wryly. "Which doesn't mean a damn thing. S'pose she's famous."

"In the art world, a bit. She's also sort of family."

He glanced back at Delia and saw her holding out the cup and saucer.

"Tea?" Her gaze was fixed on the cup. "Just a warning, but knowing Montrose like I do, it's probably chamomile or something like it at this hour."

Mac was genuinely uninterested in tea of any kind, but he took the cup and saucer from her. The fine china felt as delicate as it looked.

"You must rate pretty well with Montrose," she added. "He never serves *me* the special cookies." She selected a lavender-colored one and bit off half. She made a soft sound in her throat as she swallowed. "He makes them from scratch. And I can't tell you how much I'd like to say otherwise, but they are divine." The tip of her tongue snuck out to capture an invisible crumb before she popped the rest of the cookie in her mouth.

She made that soft sound again.

Divine.

Mac turned away as he drank half the teacup's contents. It tasted like tepid daisies—or what he imagined they'd taste like if he ever had a reason to chew on them—but it did the job of drowning the sudden knot in his throat.

He'd done the job he'd come for. Returned the wallet. Time to go.

The cup rattled in the saucer only a little when he set it on the coffee table. When he turned around again, she was standing right behind him, the small, tiered server held carefully in her hands as if she were as worried about breaking it as he was the cup and saucer.

"The lavender are my favorite. Pink have a hint of rose water. The yellow are Meyer lemon." Her gaze skipped around like a curious bee. "Don't ask me how Meyer lemon differs from other lemons, but they must, or Montrose wouldn't continually correct me about it."

He didn't want a cookie. He wanted her.

He grabbed the first cookie his blind fingers encountered and sat his butt on the couch before he reached for her instead.

"Rose water." She sounded surprised. "Not exactly what I would have guessed."

He'd grabbed a pink one, he realized. "Curious what it tastes like," he said abruptly. It wasn't exactly a lie. It just wasn't the taste of the cookie he wanted to explore.

She leaned over to place the dessert stand on the coffee table and he felt engulfed in her soft scent.

He stuffed the entire pink disc in his mouth and picked up the teacup again, washing the cookie down so fast his tastebuds couldn't keep up.

"Those supposed to be more artwork or what?" He nodded at the three violins displayed beneath the glass surface of the coffee table.

"Just violins. Vivian's father was a violin maker." She sank smoothly down onto her knees next to the coffee table and propped an elbow on the glass. "I think Casey is the only one in the family who plays, though. Have you ever heard him?"

"Only thing I've known him to play are the pool tables in Colbys." Mac had learned the hard way never to bet against him.

Her eyes smiled. "He's really good, actually."

"When does he even have a chance to play? Weaver doesn't exactly have an orchestra." None he'd heard of.

"Sometimes he does stuff with the music programs at the schools. And then. You know. Weddings." She dropped her hand suddenly and pushed to her feet. "Want a tour of the house?"

He couldn't care less about the house.

"Most people do when they come here." She tugged down the hem of her T-shirt and then her sleeves.

It dawned on him that she was nervous.

"A tour would be great."

"Well." She grabbed a yellow cookie with one hand and swept out her other in an encompassing motion that she embellished with a tiny curtsy. "You and the library have already met."

He smiled slightly and took a few cookies for himself before following her out of the room.

She showed him the formal living room that was larger than his entire childhood home. From the ceiling to the floor, the room seemed cast in gold. Museum-like. He couldn't imagine kicking back on the ivory-upholstered couch with the gilded wood arms and watching a football game.

He nodded toward the grand piano. It was as different from the scarred upright that sat in his mom's living room as a piano could get. "Do you play?"

"Nope." Her fingertips trailed over the gold-flecked wallpaper as she led the way into a smaller room. "Study, meet Mac. Mac, meet the study."

"What's the difference between a study and a library?"

"Where Vivian's concerned?" She propped her hands on her hips, looking around the room as if for the first time. "I honestly don't know. But I like this room a lot more than the library."

So did he. The books crammed every which way on these built-in shelves were mismatched and looked like they'd actually been read. And the leather couch didn't look inhospitable.

"Next up are the dining rooms." She led the way and he followed. He was having a devil of a time not ogling everything.

Her in particular.

"Dining *rooms*? As in more than one?"

She sent him an impish smile. "Welcome to Vivvie's world."

"Your world, too."

"Hardly." She pushed open a door. "Dining room

number one. For the formal events. State dinners. Christmas Balls." Her lips twisted slightly. "The dropping of unexpected family announcements."

"Could fit a couple of bowling alley lanes in there."

"Right?"

From there, they visited the *in*formal dining room. Terrifically modest. Maybe one bowling lane would fit.

After that was an entirely different breakfast room—still too fancy for Mac, but at least not sized for fifty people—and then the commercial kitchen where Montrose was sitting on a high stool.

As soon as they entered, he swiftly closed the cover on his tablet computer and stood. He gave Delia a cool look through the half glasses perched on his hooked nose.

"Montrose doesn't like anyone getting in his domain," Delia told Mac. "Isn't that right, Montrose?"

"I mind some more than others."

Delia grinned, obviously unfazed by the man's attitude.

She tucked her hand around Mac's arm and pulled him through the doorway again. "We'll let you get back to your soap opera," she said just before the door shut behind them.

Mac still heard Montrose's furious "Stay *out* of *my* kitchen!"

"I caught him watching a *Downton Abbey* rerun the other day." She looked almost gleeful as she hurried Mac into a second, smaller kitchen. "I just *know* he's hooked. I mean, who isn't?"

"I suppose I shouldn't be surprised that a house with two dining rooms would have two kitchens. But…why?"

"This one is where we lesser mortals are allowed to wallow." She opened the refrigerator as she passed it and pulled out a bottle of green juice. "Want one?"

"About as much as I want more chamomile tea."

She chuckled softly and returned the bottle to the shelf.

They left kitchen number two and passed a door that she didn't open. "Montrose's private rooms," she told him. "Even I leave him to some privacy. Not that he returns the favor. The man always seems to be in my business."

She turned down a wide hallway and passed an impressively wide staircase but didn't take it. "Bunch of bedrooms," she said to him with a wave of her hand. "And my grandmother's suite."

Was Delia's bedroom up there, too?

"Must have a lot of bedrooms in a place this big." And wondering which one was hers was a good way to drive a man insane.

"She started with seven but she's up to twelve now," Delia informed him. "And that doesn't include her suite."

"She aiming to be a hotel?"

She smiled. "Vivvie likes building."

"Why?"

She shrugged as they entered a plant-filled double-story atrium. "I don't think there's ever any explaining my grandmother." She pressed a switch and directional light flooded two opposing staircases that curved to an upper balcony encircling the entire space.

"Actually," she trailed her fingers over the scrolled back of a cushioned bench before moving to the silvery fern behind it, "that's not true." She slid her hand beneath one of the long fronds and lifted it carefully away from the bench. "I think she keeps building because she's afraid if she stops, it'll mean that she's done."

"With what?"

Her lips curved. Sadly. "Everything."

She was suddenly the woman from New Year's Eve. Heartbreaking and beautiful. "Delia."

She shook her head and cleared her throat as she rounded the bench. She perched on the cushion and crossed her legs primly. "So what do you think?" Her voice was deliberately bright.

He thought he'd never wanted a candy cane until now.

It was cooler in the atrium than the rest of the house, but only slightly. A feat considering nearly every wall was made of glass. Maybe all the plants created heat. Everywhere he looked, pots were bursting with tropical plants. There was even a palm tree.

In a mansion.

In Weaver.

What did he think? "Nice atrium." Understatement of the year.

"Con*serv*atory," Delia corrected with a drawl. Then she smiled, genuine humor returning to her expression. "My grandmother's term."

"It's a trip whatever you call it." The roof wasn't entirely glass but the part that was met in a sharp peak at the center of the room. Probably designed that way to keep snow from building up on the glass.

Right now, it was a clear night, and the bright white half-moon was plainly visible. "What's up the stairs?"

She popped off the bench and padded to the base of the staircase nearest him. "Vivian's office. My office. Well. My office until I move into my new one at the rec center." She clasped her fingers around the filigreed railing and started up the steps. "I'll miss the view. It's spectacular. You can see all the way to the lights at Angel's Flight resort."

No way that view would be better than the one he had of her climbing the stairs in front of him. "What you're really saying is the Rasmussen Automotive sign isn't as appealing?"

She sent him a smile over her shoulder.

Heiress, he reminded himself.

They reached the top and she pointed out Vivian's office but entered the darkened one next to it. He knew immediately why she didn't turn on a light. Beyond the huge window that formed the far wall, the snowy landscape was illuminated perfectly by the moonlight.

She walked right up to the window and rested her fingers lightly on the glass. "Montrose will love me for the fingerprints. As if he's ever been personally responsible for cleaning them."

"Who does that?"

"An ever-revolving team of housekeepers. None of them can stand Montrose for long."

Mac could make out the shapes of a desk situated to face out the window and some sort of small couch. But it was her figure outlined in moonlight that held his attention. "So you were your grandmother's personal assistant?"

"Mm-hmm. Not exactly rocket science-level work. Which meant I was perfect for it. And now…"

The office wasn't particularly large, and he knocked his knee into the corner of something hard as he went closer to the window. To her.

He made himself stop more than an arm's length away and fisted his hands in the pockets of his jeans. "And now?"

"Now I'm so far in over my head it's terrifying," she said softly. Then she rubbed her fingers through her hair, making it even messier. "Sorry. Tour's free and for tonight only we're tossing in confession time." Her voice was light. She tapped the window with her index finger. "I told you the lights were visible from here."

He stopped inches behind her and lifted his hand to rest on the window next to hers. Just above their fingers he could see the glimmer of golden light high on the mountain. "I've only been there to pick up a tow." Her hand was narrow. Her fingers long. His hand next to hers looked as graceful as a bear paw. "You?"

She shifted and her shoulder touched his chest. Fleetingly. "Not really any reason to go there. If I want to play at being a cowgirl, I don't need a guest ranch to do it when I have plenty of cousins around with real ranches."

Angel's Flight wasn't just a fancy dude ranch. It was a high-end ski resort. "What about skiing?"

"I'm more the hot toddy by the fireplace type. Or haven't you figured that out?"

"The only thing I've figured out where you're concerned is that I haven't figured you out at all."

"Join the club," she murmured.

He jerked his head back up when he realized he was damn close to burying his nose in her thick, wavy hair. "Were you in bed when I got here?"

"My jammies give me away?"

"And you thought I was Stewart."

Her shoulders stiffened against his chest. "So?"

The office was small in relation to every other room on the tour, but it wasn't that small. If she wanted to move away from him, she could.

She didn't.

Her skin was warm when he moved his thumb from the windowpane and grazed it over the back of her hand. "You meet all your business associates in your jammies?"

"Every single one."

"Liar."

She shook her head and her hair rippled. "Then why'd you ask?"

"Just making sure. I don't play in other people's fields."

"I could ask the same of you."

"I have no jammies." Literally.

"And your…field?" Her voice was soft. Her thumb rubbed against his. "No associates?"

"Business or otherwise." He moved his hand, covering hers. "Have you finished your homework?"

She curled her fingers, pushing the back of her hand against his palm. "What homework?"

When he slid her wavy hair away from her cheek, it was as soft and silky as he'd imagined. "Best practices," he reminded against her ear.

"Oh, that." She shifted against him and tilted her head when he kissed the side of her neck. "I'll get to it at…ah…at some point."

He reached her shoulder, hooking his finger beneath the soft stretchy stripes, and slid the fabric aside enough to kiss her bare skin.

She inhaled deeply and flattened her other hand against the window, too.

He slid the shirt an inch further. "I don't want to be responsible for you not—"

"You really want to talk?" She arched against him.

"When you put it that way." He slid his arm around her waist, his fingers splayed on her belly, pulling her in against him more closely.

She tilted her head back against his chest, swaying slightly, and made that divine sound in her throat.

She straightened her hand beneath his against the window and spread her fingers.

"Mac."

He slid his fingers between hers. "Hmm?"

She rubbed the back of her head back and forth beneath his chin. "Just… Mac," she said on a husky sigh.

He ran his thumb up over the jut of her breast. Soft. Firm. He found her tight nipple and she arched even more.

He kissed her neck again. "Where's your room?"

"West wing." She rocked against him. "Too far."

He let out a rough breath, pressed his head against her shoulder and found control from somewhere.

Wallet. The only reason he'd gone there that night.

He got his hand back to the safety of her waist. "Right." He pushed out the gruff word and straightened.

But she grabbed his hand. "I didn't mean I wanted to stop."

Blood was raging inside him. "I'm too old for games."

"So am I." She drew his hand back to her belly. Beneath the shirt. "Touch me," she whispered.

"Where?"

She cupped his hand to her breast. It was bare beneath the shirt. Velvety smooth and warm. Against the window, her fingers slid down through his.

"Everywhere," she breathed.

He let out a long, long breath.

And he touched her. Just as she touched him.

Everywhere. Right there against the window in the moonlight.

And after, she took him by the hand and they walked through the house. Up the wide staircase and down one hall after another until she finally stopped in front of a closed door.

He looked up and down the hallway. "West wing?"

She went on her toes and kissed his jaw. "Told you it was too far." Then she pushed open the door and with a soft smile on her face pulled him inside her bedroom.

Chapter Thirteen

"You're looking very chipper this morning."

Delia slipped into her chair at the breakfast table. She was still feeling euphoric, but she calmly reached for a palmier from the tray. She gave her grandmother a glance. "Am I?"

Vivian was peering at her over the tops of her reading glasses. She had a folded newspaper next to one elbow and a plate of cut fruit in front of her. "Dare I say it has to do with the company of a certain gentleman?"

Montrose.

Delia silently cursed the man. There was no way her grandmother would know about Mac's visit unless Montrose had told her. Delia had walked Mac out to his truck herself long before the sun had even come up.

Yes, she'd felt a little like a teenager sneaking in and out after curfew, but she didn't regret a second of the time they'd spent together even if he hadn't said a word about seeing her again…

Her grandmother was still waiting, her eyebrows raised.

"Maybe," Delia allowed.

She picked up the gold coffeepot and carefully tipped the long spout over her cup. It had taken living with Vivian for nearly four years, but she'd finally mastered the art of pouring from the vintage coffeepot without splashing coffee everywhere.

"I had a feeling." Vivian looked pleased. At least until Delia dunked the corner of her palmier in her coffee cup. Then she sighed faintly and lifted the newspaper. "Have you delivered all of my invitations?"

"I didn't make it up to Angel's Flight yet." Delia nearly squirmed in her seat, the memory of Mac's hand over hers as they'd looked up at the mountain still fresh.

"You'll have to go up there today," Vivian said. "Rory tells me they're heading back to Denver tomorrow."

For a man like Gage who had his own private jet, the distance between Denver and Weaver was a minor detail. "If you were talking to Gage's wife, why not just tell her about your little do?"

"Because even in this day and age, it's important to use proper invitations for such things."

In Vivian's world, perhaps. "I promise I'll drive up there today," she said.

"Thank you. Ah!" Vivian's smile widened and she set aside her newspaper when Stewart entered the breakfast room. "Good morning, dear." A smile hovered around her lips. "You're looking dapper as ever."

Dapper. Code for three-piece suit.

Stewart seemed to have a never-ending supply of them. He'd been in Weaver for weeks and Delia hadn't really noticed any repeats.

"And you're looking as lovely as always, Vivian." Stewart took a plate from the sideboard and studied the selections before settling on a scoop of fluffy scrambled eggs.

Delia didn't even have to look to know that he'd also choose three slices of beefsteak tomato and three cubes of cantaloupe. The same thing he had every morning.

She dunked her palmier and wondered what Mac liked to eat for breakfast. So far, she knew he was a steak lover the same as her.

And that he had a ticklish spot on the small of his back.

Her mind immediately drifted back into delicious places—

"Have you finished the articles?" Stewart set his plate on the table and took the seat beside her.

She childishly crossed her fingers beneath the linen tablecloth. "Yes."

She *had* been reading Stewart's articles the night before when Montrose had told her she was needed in the library. Since that was where Stewart usually spent his evenings before retiring to the guesthouse, she'd gone down expecting him to grill her over what she'd learned from them.

Only she'd found Mac.

And now, the morning after, her blood was singing in her veins and the copies of Stewart's precious articles were still strewn all over her bedroom floor.

"What did you think?"

That he had the most confident hands she'd ever met.

She realized that Vivian was watching her with an unusually indulgent expression.

"Fascinating." She quickly changed the subject. "I dropped off the employment forms for Charmaine Macdonald, by the way."

"Good." He spread his napkin precisely on his lap. "I think she's the best we can hope for right now."

The edge of her pastry crumbled off into her coffee. "You seemed a big enough fan of her the other day." She fished the sodden bit out with her spoon. "Something change?"

"Not at all. Considering the pool we're working with here, she rose above them all."

She tucked her tongue behind her teeth for a moment. "The pool we're working with meaning what?

The people who applied so far? Or the bumpkins of Weaver in general?"

"Delia, dear," Vivian chided. "Stewart isn't casting aspersions on the quality of our community. Now. When is Ms. Macdonald coming on board?"

"Monday." Delia noticed how Stewart didn't deny casting aspersions. He merely continued cutting his tomato slices into perfectly proportioned wedges. "You should come by then. Meet her and see our progress."

"Excellent idea." Stewart nodded with approval. "Vivian, did you speak with my father yesterday? He mentioned he was going to call."

"Yes." Vivian didn't have a chance to elaborate because Montrose entered and leaned over her, murmuring softly. Then he straightened and left the room again in his ponderously measured way.

"You'll have to excuse me, I'm afraid." Vivian dabbed her lips with her napkin before rising.

Delia eyed her grandmother closely. "Is everything all right?"

"Right as rain." Vivian waved her hand slightly, encompassing them both. Her brown eyes looked alarmingly mischievous. "You two youngsters enjoy your time together. As if you need any encouragement on that score."

Stewart looked at Delia after Vivian left the room. "What was that about?"

"No idea," she lied.

Montrose had obviously not said anything about Mac because it seemed abundantly clear to Delia that Vivian thought her matchmaking efforts where Stewart was concerned were working.

She didn't see her grandmother the rest of the morning.

Not that she had any plan to correct Vivian's misapprehension where Stewart was concerned.

A Vivian who believed a plan was working was a Vivian who quickly moved on to her next project.

Soon after her grandmother had left, Delia also excused herself and returned to her bedroom.

She would have liked to throw herself down on the bed to savor every memory of Mac, but instead, she restored the wrinkled pages of Stewart's articles to some semblance of order. She scanned through them as well as she could before her phone vibrated reminding her of the video meeting with the web designer. They did it in the library on Stewart's laptop. Afterward, the two of them scheduled more interviews for the rec center and then—per usual—Stewart took himself off to deal with his own matters.

Which left her free to drive up to Angel's Flight and deliver the last invitation.

She stopped in town for gas, since her fuel gauge was nearly empty, and smiled to herself when she spotted Mac's tow truck turning down a side street near the sheriff's station. She thought about calling him. But he was working. Not doing something irrelevant like hand-delivering a party invitation.

With her gas tank full, she hit the highway and left the town behind.

If the route between Weaver and Braden was considered dicey, then the hairpin turns driving up the side of Rambling Mountain surely qualified as treacherous, even though every single turn presented a driver with a spectacular view of the ranch valley below.

The road straightened out a good bit before she reached the series of picturesque horse barns that stepped their way up the steep incline before the actual resort came into view.

Even thinking she was prepared for it, Delia couldn't keep from catching her breath at the sight.

Built into the side of the mountain with an enormous deck that cantilevered right over the cliffside, the lodge looked like something out of a movie.

She parked and went inside where the view was even more spectacular. In some clever way, it felt like the sky was reaching right into the lodge.

Well done, Nick.

She was watching a bird swoop then suddenly soar high in the sky, as if it were dancing on the wind, when a young woman approached, asking if she needed assistance.

Delia flicked a glance at her tasteful name badge. "Hi, Willow. I'm Delia Templeton. I need to drop this off—" she lifted the envelope "—with Gage Stanton if he's available."

"I'll check for you. Is this your first time here?"

"I guess you can tell, what with my gaping expression?"

Willow had a winning smile. "It's a familiar look

on everyone's face when they come here for the first time." She gestured toward the cozy groupings of chairs arranged around the stunning room. "Have a seat and I'll check on Gage."

"Thanks." Delia waited until the other woman had left before she wandered closer to the windows.

Seen from the mansion, Angel's Flight had been only a gleam of golden light in the dark. There was little likelihood that the mansion would be visible from the resort.

That didn't stop Delia from trying to spot it, anyway.

"My wife tells me we need a telescope."

She whirled around to see Gage walking toward her. He was tall. Dark-haired. Dark-eyed. He was also the spitting image of the photos Vivian had of Thatcher. Gage was older, of course, because his father had still been a young man when he'd died, leaving behind the woman he'd loved and their toddler son. But the resemblance was plain.

"She's right," Delia said. "The view's incredible. Well. All of it's incredible. You must be very proud of it." She extended the envelope. "Vivian is having one of her soirees week after next."

He took the envelope. "And what's this?"

"The invitation. Which I was instructed to hand-deliver." A task she'd now completed. "It's basically just a family get-together when she has an excuse to put away her everyday diamonds for the really special stuff and Montrose can break out the *good* caviar."

He smiled slightly. "In my world, we do get-togethers with a cookout and a keg."

She knew Gage's world was a lot more sophisticated than he claimed but she still chuckled. "We have that in common, then. Vivian likes thinking she's bringing culture and sophistication into our lives."

"One soiree at a time apparently."

"I know it would mean a lot to her if you and Rory could make it."

"And Killian and Thea? Rory's not going to want to leave her and I'm guessing Vivian's aiming at just the adults with this." He flicked the envelope between his fingers.

"Honestly, Gage, I don't think Vivian would care if you showed up with a school bus full of children as long as you're there. It's just a few hours on a Friday night." She knew Vivian's little parties. They rarely lasted more than two or three hours. "So? Will you come?"

He looked resigned as he nodded.

Delia was relieved. He hadn't attended the New Year's brunch and she hadn't been certain which way his particular chip would fall this time. "All right, then." She flipped her scarf around her throat again. "I'm sure you're busy, so I won't keep you any lon—" She broke off at the sight of several horseback riders outside making their way in a single file down a crevice in the rocks.

Gage noticed. "They're heading down to Lambert Lake."

Delia cleared her throat. "Looks dangerous."

"Megan doesn't let the horses get into danger." He looked wry. "I think keeping the riders out of danger too is just a byproduct of that."

"Her baby's only a few weeks older than Thea. I didn't think she'd be back to work already."

"Who're we talking about?" Rory came up behind Gage. She had a brilliantly colored scarf wrapped around her torso that Delia was pretty sure contained baby Thea.

"Megan and her horses."

"Ah." Rory nodded with understanding but when she looked at Delia there was a hint of reserve in her eyes.

Loyal to her BFF, no doubt.

Megan had probably told her all about Delia's failed pursuit of Nick.

"Well." Delia began edging sideways. "Until Vivian's party, then." Gage could do whatever explaining was necessary to his wife.

"Until then."

She left.

Maybe she was a little too glad that she hadn't encountered Megan, but a girl *did* have her pride.

Her phone rang just as she reached the main highway again.

She unclenched her fingers and glanced at the display. She didn't know the number or the name and she hit the button on her steering wheel to send the call to her voice mail.

"Four hundred and eleven," she muttered and

thought maybe she ought to turn off the automatic notifications that told her how many entries had been made at *WEAVERFUNDS*.

Sometimes she really missed the days when there'd been no cell phone service around Weaver at all.

She drove back toward town but passed the turn-off to Vivian's.

She wondered if Mac would come to the party if she invited him.

Slow down, girl. You don't even know if last night was a onetime thing or not.

She proved her self-control by not turning in at his garage. Instead she drove past it and continued straight to Classic Charms. At the very least, her self-control deserved a little retail reward.

She went inside, telling herself that said reward did not necessarily entail sexy lingerie.

Still, she slowed down as she neared the old-fashioned telephone booth with a headless mannequin positioned inside. But instead of the usual display of panties hanging indolently from the mannequin's arms, a child's mobile dangled from one hand and a pastel green-and-yellow quilt from the other.

"Hi, Delia." Jennifer, the salesclerk stopped next to her. "What do you think?" she asked, indicating the new display.

"Cute." Delia had plenty of sexy lingerie languishing in drawers, but she didn't have baby gifts for her cousins. If she bought them now, she wouldn't have to do so later when the babies arrived. She reached into the phone booth to turn over the tiny price tag on the blanket and nearly choked.

"I figure we'll see more baby stuff than usual for a while," Jennifer commented.

"Why is that?" Delia let go of the price tag. How could a baby-sized quilt be so expensive?

"Sydney's pregnant. I would have thought you heard the news."

Sydney was married to one of Squire's grandsons. And so there was yet another family baby in the works. Delia hoped her smile didn't look as forced as it felt. "That's great." She pulled off her short coat and bunched it under her arm.

Jennifer wound up the mobile and set it into motion. The dangling moons and stars slowly turned while a soft lullaby played. "I put my name in on your website," she said softly. As if she didn't want anyone to hear.

Delia raised her eyebrows and waited. She had plenty of practice with it by now.

"I want to open my own business," Jennifer whispered. "Selling custom-made dog biscuits—" She glanced toward the door when the bell above it jangled softly. A delivery person was entering with a stack of boxes. Looking reluctant, Jennifer excused herself to deal with it.

Delia escaped, quickly aiming for the far side of the store where the women's clothing was located. She never knew what treasures she might find on the spinning racks but when she reached the area, she stopped in surprise at the sight of Hayley standing by one of them, browsing through the selections.

"Seth said you weren't supposed to be on your feet these days," Delia said in greeting.

Hayley jumped and pressed her hand to her chest. "You startled me."

"Better me than your husband finding you're out shopping. How'd you escape his eagle eye anyway?"

"He had a little emergency at work." She chewed the inside of her cheek for a second. "You don't have to mention running into me when you see him."

Delia laughed. "Dangerous to put *those* cards in my hand." She angled a look at her cousin's pregnant figure. "Surprised someone's not running a pool on you and Ali. Betting on when you deliver."

"Someone is." J.D. Forrest stepped out from behind the velvet curtain of the fitting room carrying a pair of jeans. "The twins got it going. Because, naturally, that is what every pair of eighteen-year-olds do. Selling two chances a day at twenty-five bucks a pop per mama until the twenty-first of the month."

"Why the twenty-first?"

"Induce day," Hayley said. "For me, anyway." She made a face. "Ali's two days earlier."

"Either way, nobody's going past then." J.D. folded the jeans and placed them back on the display shelf.

"No good?" Hayley asked.

J.D. rubbed her hands down her hips. "Can I blame it on childbirth even though my youngest is nearly ten?"

Delia and Hayley exchanged droll looks. The other woman was as long-legged and as lean as her youngest son. "I should only be so lucky." Delia began sifting through the hangers. "I haven't worn a size four since I was in junior high. How many chances have they sold so far?"

"No idea. Winner takes all, so it's 2100 smackers if they sell them all. They started the first day of the month."

Delia looked at Hayley, then at J.D. "Is there still room to get in on it?"

"Honestly," Hayley chided and awkwardly sat down in an upholstered slipper chair near the changing room. She blew out a breath and brushed her blond hair away from her face.

"You'll have to ask them," J.D. said. "Jake and I take no part in their betting activities." Her eyes were full of laughter because at one point, her husband had raised and raced thoroughbred horses. Now, they ran a huge horse rescue called Crossing West. "But I've gotta say—" she was eyeing Hayley "—I'm kind of wishing I'd picked tomorrow."

"I'm not having the baby tomorrow," Hayley said dismissively.

She sounded halfhearted, but who was Delia to judge?

She pulled a royal blue sheath off the rack to get a better look. It was sleeveless with a wide square neckline. She'd still be able to wear a bra. It was also longer than she usually liked though it did have a healthy slit up one side.

The style would suit her. But it was the color that was the striking part.

"That's pretty," Hayley said.

She stuck it back on the rack. Buying a dress because the color reminded her of Mac's eyes was dangerously sentimental.

"Oh." Hayley pouted a little. "Really? I think the color's gorgeous."

Delia lifted her shoulder. "No bling." She nudged the dress until she could see the price tag. Not baby-quilt level, but not inexpensive, either. Even marked down to half price the way it was.

"A figure like yours needs no bling." J.D. sounded a little grumpy about it.

Delia brushed past her and crouched in front of the stacks of jeans. She finally pulled out a pair and pushed them into J.D.'s hands. "Try those."

"I'd listen to her," Hayley advised. "She's got a weird sixth sense about that sort of thing."

J.D. went back into the fitting room and closed the curtain again. "How's the rec center coming along?" she said from inside.

"Good." Delia went back to flipping through the hangers on the circle rack. "We still need to fill several positions, but Charmaine Macdonald starts Monday as the new manager." She plucked a shirt from the rack and pushed it past the curtain. "Try that, too."

"It's got sequins. I'm too old for sequins."

"Oh for—" J.D. was only four years older than

Delia. "Nobody's too old for sequins." She wiggled the hanger insistently until she felt J.D. take it from her.

"What kind of positions?" Hayley asked. "J.D. was just saying that the boys were looking for jobs to tide them over until college starts in the fall."

"Really?" She knew the other woman's twin stepsons had always worked at Crossing West.

"Really." J.D.'s head popped out around the corner of the curtain. "Just so they'll have something else on their résumés besides working for me. But they have a reputation as being pretty rowdy around town." Her head disappeared again. "Rightfully so," she added somewhat grimly.

"High energy," Hayley corrected. "Which hasn't stopped them from achieving good grades."

"High energy at a rec center is a good thing," Delia told them. She took two more blouses from the rack and pushed them beyond the curtain. "As for the sort of jobs available? Take your pick. Equipment room attendant. After-school care attendant. Craft instructor. Basically, everything from staffing the front desk to lifeguarding the pool." She spun the rack and slid some more hangers around. "Some positions like lifeguard need special certifications, obviously, but every staff member will have a security check. And a lot of the positions have crossover depending on the skill level and hours availa—*what*?"

Both Hayley and J.D.—who'd poked out her head again—were giving her looks.

Hayley gave an innocent shrug. "Nothing. Just don't always see you so…" She trailed off, obviously hunting for her words, which for Hayley was not a usual occurrence.

"I was rowdy too." Delia pointed at her with the hanger she was holding. "And when I was Zach and Connor's age, I couldn't have cared less about going to college." Much to her parents' dismay. She stuck the hanger back on the rack and pulled a padded one off that held a chunky black sweater. With J.D.'s fair coloring it would be spectacular.

"I can tell you right now, J.D., they have a job. They'll have to follow the same rules as every other employee. If for some reason it doesn't work out— which I don't think will happen—but if it does, then hopefully they'll still have learned something positive from the experience." She realized she was waving around the sweater and stuck it through the curtain.

"You know I *did* just come in here for some jeans." J.D. whipped the curtain aside and preened a little in the pair that Delia had given her. They hugged her rear like a lover and the soft teal sequin T-shirt added just the right amount of casual bling.

"Told you," Hayley said. "Weird."

Delia ignored her. "I actually have some employment packets in my car ready to go. The boys can fill them out immediately."

"Sounds perfect." J.D. was craning around trying to see the reflection of her backside. "They don't look too tight?"

"I hate you a little bit right now," Hayley grumbled.

Delia ran out to her car and returned with two of

the packets that she handed over to J.D., who had exchanged the sequins for the black sweater. "Charmaine really is the one who's going to be in charge there," she said. "I mean she's the manager."

J.D. took the packets and tossed them onto the little bench that she'd piled with clothes. When she turned back, she gave Delia a quick hug. "This is great, Delia. Seriously." Then she stepped back and laughed as she looked at the clothes. "Mama's buying herself a little bling."

"Gotta pee," Hayley said abruptly and began struggling to her feet. Delia quickly took her arm, helping her stand.

Hayley puffed a little and waddled away, one hand pressed to her back.

"She's having that baby before Ali." Delia watched her go. "I just saw her yesterday and she was still bouncing around with all the energy in the world." She pulled out her cell phone. "Do the twins have cell phones?" She glanced back at J.D.

Her cousin had her own phone at her ear already. "Connor? Put me down for tomorrow." J.D.'s eyes danced. "Noon-to-midnight." She held her hand over the phone. "Midnight to noon's already taken," she said.

"By whom?"

"Seth."

Delia ended up taking the only two chances still available. The noon-to-midnight for Ali on the coming Wednesday. And the midnight-to-noon on the last day of the pool for Hayley.

For her cousins' sakes, she hoped they didn't have to wait that long. But on the highly unlikely chance that Delia did win?

She could buy the pastel quilt.

Two of them.

They all left with Classic Charms shopping bags in their hands. Delia with two newborn outfits she'd purchased while Hayley was still waddling back from the bathroom. J.D. with three bags holding everything that Delia had suggested. Hayley with a heart-shaped box of chocolates that she'd already broken into.

Delia walked her to her car. "You let me know when you're home, okay?"

"I will."

She waited until her cousin's SUV was out of sight and went back into the store.

She bought the royal blue dress.

It was only sensible, she reasoned. It *had* been on sale.

After that, she stopped in at the corner drugstore and bought a couple of gift bags and tissue paper for the baby outfits, spending twice as much as she would have had she driven to the other side of town to Shop-World.

Then she drove to Mac's garage.

Self-control was overrated.

It was after five but the middle bay door was open and she could see a car inside up on jacks.

She parked near the office and peered inside the window. Loreen was still at her desk and she leaned over to unlock the door when she spotted Delia. "Come on in. Problems with the car?" She didn't wait for Delia to answer. "Mac," she said into the intercom and the echo of it practically bounced off the walls. "Got a sec for the Porsche?"

Delia tried again. "Actually, my car is—" Through the window, she saw Mac straighten from the engine. His blue, blue gaze met hers and he smiled slowly. "Fine," she finished absently.

"Well, well, well," she heard Loreen say but the words didn't really penetrate. In fact, nothing really sank in until she saw Loreen in her coat and hat closing the office door after herself.

The closed sign in the window blinked on, bright red.

Chapter Fourteen

"So." Mac stopped in the doorway between the garage and the office. "Problem with the car?"

Self-control was overrated but bravery was a tougher nut. "Yes," she lied. Then shook her head. Old Delia was gone. "No. Car's fine. I wanted to see you." She moistened her lips. "I realize we didn't say anything about…that."

A faint smile played about his lips. "We didn't, did we."

"So…" She walked over to him, not stopping until her boots bumped his. "What do you think?"

His hands settled lightly on her hips. "I wanted to see you, too."

Elation filled her. "Oh yeah?" She toyed with the zipper of his coverall.

His smile widened. "You don't answer your phone enough. I left you two messages." His fingers flexed and he pulled her an inch closer. "Just so you know, I've had a helluva time concentrating today. Haven't accomplished a damn thing."

"Really?" She inched the zipper down a few inches. Enough to reveal the plain white T-shirt beneath. "Strangely enough, I've had a surprisingly productive day." She flicked a glance up at his face. "I could take off my coat," she pulled the zipper down even further and grazed her knuckles over his abdomen, "and stay a while."

"Or," he trapped her hand and dropped a brief kiss on her lips, "I could lock up down here and we go upstairs."

She knew that was his home. She leaned in to kiss him, a little less briefly. "Upstairs."

"Good decision."

She batted her eyelashes. "I've been full of them today."

He laughed outright. "Tell me those aren't real eyelashes."

She poked an indignant finger into his belly. It was like poking a cement block. "Yes, my eyelashes are real. But even if they weren't, if a person wants to add a little help in the lash department who cares, if it makes her feel good?"

He looped his arm around her shoulder. "You make me feel good," he murmured and kissed her again.

She was melting inside. And that was only partially because she was still wearing her coat.

Just when she was about ready to pull him with

her over to Loreen's counter-style desk, he let go of her. "Ten minutes to lock up," he promised.

It took him five.

Holding her hand, he tugged her outside and around to the staircase on the back of the building. "Careful. Steps get icy."

He hadn't bothered to put on a coat for the short trip and she enjoyed the rear view of him as she lagged several steps behind him. The only time she glanced away was to look at her phone and read the text message from Hayley that she was home.

He reached the top and unlocked the door, giving her a quizzical look. "Changed your mind?"

She smiled and took the rest of the stairs more quickly. "Never," she said as she ducked under his arm where he was holding the door and went inside. Her first impression was of a big TV on one wall. Couch in front of it. Kitchen on another wall. Small round table and two chairs. The books crammed into the narrow bookcase were the only things that looked even slightly disorderly.

"Ever been in a garage apartment before?" Standing behind her, he drew off her coat and hung it on one of the wall pegs next to the door.

"Yes, as a matter of fact." She smiled over her shoulder at him. "Tommy Bodecker. Sixth grade. His daddy had one he liked to rent out."

"If he was renting it out, what were you and Tommy Bodecker doing there?"

"Learning how to kiss mostly." She fluffed her hair.

"Well, aside from sixth-grade girls being too young for that, you learned your lessons very well."

"Clearly, your sixth grade wasn't like mine." She slid her hand behind his neck. "And I wish I'd learned all my lessons as well. Technically speaking, we were supposed to be cleaning the place out between renters."

He chuckled and covered her mouth with his.

She was almost swaying on her feet when he finally broke the kiss and lifted his head.

No question, he'd been an excellent student in the field of kissing himself.

"So." His eyes were lazy and definitely just as blue as the dress she'd purchased. He drew her hair away from her face and tucked it slowly behind her ear. "Want a tour of the house?"

"Yes, please."

He closed his hands over her shoulders and turned her around again. "Apartment, meet Delia." He swept his hand in front of her. "Delia, meet Apartment."

She laughed, delighted, and turned in his arms. Happiness was bubbling in her veins. She caught his face in her hands and kissed him.

"You're missing the rest of the tour," he said against her lips.

"We'll get to it," she said against his.

They did.

But it took a while.

"Okay." Delia sat in the middle of his bed wearing nothing but his discarded T-shirt. "Go through this again. I think I've almost got it."

Mac was sprawled on his stomach. He pressed

his mouth against her bare thigh and pointed at each of the faces in the photograph, going left to right. "Dev's the oldest." He covered the next face with his thumb. "Don't know who that turkey is."

"You were so young. *Macnair.*" She rubbed her fingers through his thick hair. It was darker blond now than in the picture and much shorter. "Such a pretty little boy."

"I beg your pardon." He gave her the stink eye. "I'm fourteen in that picture. Handsome. That's the word you're looking for. And *nobody* calls me Macnair. Not even my mother."

She smiled. She'd told him about her family. Now he was telling her about his. "And that's Skelly next to you. Then—"

"Kane. Egan. And the baby of the family, Adair."

"The brothers Jeffries." Raised alone by their mother, Faye, after her husband, Jack, died in a farming accident. She leaned over and kissed Mac's neck. "I'm sorry you lost your dad." He'd been ten. Dev— the oldest—twelve. And Adair just two. "And I'm sorry about your mom."

"She had it rough." He turned onto his back and pulled the framed photo off Delia's lap, holding it up where he could study it. "I get why she drank. But I can still smell the mints she always ate trying to hide the smell."

He leaned over to push the frame onto the blanket chest he used as a nightstand. "I don't begrudge people their right to drink. But it's a problem when it turns into an addiction like hers." He looked at the scar on his arm. "And when you're working around equipment that'll take your arm off if you're not careful."

His father had died when his tractor flipped. But Mac had gotten his arm nearly severed in a towing winch accident that could have been prevented if his boss at the time had been sober.

Once he recovered, he'd started saving every penny he could to go into business for himself.

He shook his head as if he were shaking off the memories. Then he turned back to kiss her knee and toss the pillow at her. "Enough laziness." He rolled off the bed, stretching. "Someone's kept me busy for the last two hours and I'm starving."

Delia caught her tongue between her teeth for a moment, absorbing the sight. "Wh-what…" She cleared her throat. He was so perfect in every single way. "What're you hungry for?"

He slid her a look that had her nerve endings singing all over again. "Rib eye was last night."

Funny, she thought. It felt like so much had happened since then. "You don't do steak two nights in a row?"

He laughed. "Babe, there've been times when I didn't do steak two years in a row." He grabbed her hand and pulled her to her feet. "Pizza Bella?"

She narrowed her eyes, studying him. "Do you eat your crusts?"

He made a face. "Hell yeah, I eat my crusts. Best part."

"Good thing you said that. I'd have to seriously

reconsider falling for someone who didn't like their pizza crusts." She heard her words after they were already out and felt her cheeks turn hot. She snuck around him to dart into the cozy bathroom first. "Five minutes. That's all I need." She shut the door right in his face.

She pressed her hands to her fiery cheeks and eyed herself in the mirror over the sink. "Subtle," she whispered and reached into the shower stall to turn on the water. The narrow space was tiled with small white squares that reminded her of the tile in the Bodecker apartment. Only she and Tommy had never gotten the grout there as white as Mac's.

She tugged the shower curtain—a blue-and-green plaid that reminded her of a particular shirt her father liked—across the rod to keep the shower spray from soaking the linoleum.

The door creaked open and she looked over her shoulder at Mac.

"There's not going to be enough hot water for us both." He stepped into the room, shrinking it even more. There was barely space to turn around.

She could pretend she hadn't blurted out those words about falling for him.

She *would* pretend.

"You have a plan in place to deal with this very situation, I assume?"

"A good plan." He whisked the shirt over her head and pitched it through the doorway toward the bed. Then he pulled the shower curtain aside just long enough to bustle her into the stall.

"Whoa!" She scrambled to get out from the cold spray, but he was stalwartly in her path. "It's freezing!"

"It'll get warm." His hands found her waist and he lifted her right off her feet, turning so his back was against the water and she was pressed against the tile. "Put your legs around me."

Even with goose bumps covering every inch of her skin, desire flooded through her. She wrapped her legs around his hips and stifled a laugh when her toes knocked into the tile behind him. "There is not enough room for this."

"There's plenty."

She caught her breath when his hand found her. Pleasure streaked through her fast and immediate. "My hair is getting soaked." She hadn't intended on having to dry her hair when pizza was so close in their future.

"You complaining?"

She shook her head, arching helplessly even though there was no room to arch. He kissed her breasts. Surrounded her nipples in warmth while the cold water sprayed over them. His fingers pressed. Slid. Sending her careening straight toward the edge.

She didn't want to go over alone. She reached between them and wrapped her hand around him. "Apparently cold water doesn't bother you."

He laughed and pressed into her. Filling her. Right up to the very heart of her.

"Plenty of room," he said again, his breath rough against her ear.

She barely heard. But oh, she felt.

Felt more than she'd ever felt in her life.

And when the water turned warm while pleasure coursed through them both, she didn't have to worry about him ever noticing the inexplicable tears that slid from the corners of her eyes.

"Anyway," Delia reached for another piece—her third—of the cheese and basil pizza. "I thought at first that Montrose had ratted me out to my grandmother." She bit off the delectably chewy tip.

On a Friday night, they'd had to wait for more than an hour for a table at Pizza Bella.

She thought she'd used the time well, blathering about Hayley and Ali and the meeting with the website designer. About anything and everything that distracted her from the shaky feeling she still had inside.

"But Montrose hadn't told her," Mac concluded.

The booths at Pizza Bella were small. Intimate. Not as intimate as Mac's shower stall, but still, they couldn't move their legs beneath the little round table without touching each other.

Thank goodness she had her emotions back in hand.

"Nope. She thinks there's something up between me and Stewart." She reached for her glass of iced tea. "It's perfect, really."

"Why's that again?"

"As long as she's focused on Stewart, she won't be looking for another explanation for my chipper mood." She grinned, belatedly noticing that Mac wasn't shoveling down his food at the same pace she was. "Are you sure you wouldn't have preferred pizza with more toppings than just basil?"

"I'm sure." His iced tea was cut in half by lemonade. A virtuous Arnold Palmer. "It's important that your grandmother doesn't know about us?"

Us. The word was like lifting the lid on a box of butterflies. She clamped it back down, but not before a whole lot of fluttering. "Vivian loves sticking her nose where she wants. Believe me. You'll thank me for protecting you from that."

"Sure you're not protecting her?"

She set down her slice of pizza. "From what?"

His lips moved in a smile that wasn't entirely a smile. "I'm a mechanic."

"One good enough to keep her Rolls-Royce going despite her best efforts. What's your point?"

"Stewart's acceptable. He'd be a good match—"

"I'm not in *love* with Stewart!" Her voice rang out.

Mac stared at her.

The hostess escorting a couple to the table next to theirs stared at her.

It felt like everyone in the entire restaurant was staring at her.

She was mortified. "I'm not in love with anyone," she muttered. "So there's no need to get all uptight about it."

He spread his fingers, suddenly looking annoyingly calm. "I'm not uptight. Are you uptight?"

"No, I'm not uptight!" She boldly met the gaze

of the woman in the booth across from her until she finally looked away.

Then Delia snatched up her pizza again. She glared a little at Mac. "Don't be smiling like that."

He raised his eyebrows. "Like what?"

She huffed and shoved a bite of pizza into her mouth. It suddenly tasted like cardboard.

She swallowed, tossed her napkin aside and excused herself. "I'm going to the ladies' room."

He stood.

She scooted past him and hurried out of the dining room.

Her cheeks looked flushed in the mirror over the restroom sink. And her eyes—

She closed them. What would Ali say about the expression in her eyes now?

"Are you all right?"

Delia curled her fingers and looked up. "I'm fine. Go ahead." She moved out of the way so the waitress could wash her hands.

"You're Delia Templeton, aren't you? I saw your picture in *The Weaver Gazette*. Are you really giving away free money?"

Delia sighed. "We'll be funding *some* charitable causes. If you have a particular need, you can submit details at our temporary website and we'll get back to you later."

After the waitress left, she washed her hands and, feeling only marginally more collected, returned to their table.

Charmaine Macdonald was sitting there with Mac. The two of them were laughing.

I'm not uptight. Right. Putting a smile on her face that didn't feel like a stretched rubber band was impossible.

She stepped up to the table. "Hi, Charmaine." She was slightly mollified when Mac stretched out his arm and caught her around the waist.

"Hey!" The other woman's brilliant hair streamed around her shoulders. "I was just telling Mac about Carmela winning the spelling bee in her class." She was beaming. "The next step is the regional bee."

"Congratulations."

"You'll be there, yeah?" Charmaine looked at Mac.

"Wouldn't miss it."

She squeezed his hand and started to slide out of the booth, holding her coat in her lap. "Mac's the best," she told Delia.

The rubber band stretched a little more.

"You don't have to leave," Mac said and glanced at Delia. "She's waiting for her takeout."

"Lot faster than trying to dine in. Wait line is halfway around the building," Charmaine said. "I came in to warm up for a minute and spotted Mac."

"When's the regional bee?" Delia asked.

"Next month. She says she doesn't expect to win, but she's studying her heart out."

"Someone's going to win," Delia said. "Why not her?"

"Exactly," Mac said. "She's the smartest twelve-year-old *I* know."

"You guys are sweet." Charmaine finally scooted out of the booth. "And I am *not* going to crash your date any longer. But I will see you first thing Monday morning," she told Delia. "Eight sharp. And hey. Stewart copied me on some of those applications. I actually know a lot of the applicants. I hope it wasn't premature of me since I don't even officially start work until Monday, but I took the liberty of scheduling a few people to come in that afternoon. I think Maia Grimes might be a perfect fit for the preschool director. She was Carmela's kindergarten teacher."

"The sooner the better. And you can blame me for being premature, too, because I already said we'd find a spot for Connor and Zach Forrest," Delia told her quickly.

"Aren't they the ones who put a snake in the principal's—you know what?" Charmaine waved a dismissive hand. "Doesn't matter. It's all going to be great."

Delia slid back into the booth when Charmaine left. "You two have been friends a long time?"

"She was my second job at Rasmussen's," he said. "Head gasket." He shook his head. "Not a good situation."

"I don't even know what a head gasket is, so I'll take your word for it." Her abandoned pizza slice was still sitting on the plate exactly where she'd left it. But her appetite had waned.

"We didn't really get to know each other, though, until Ethan broke into the garage."

She felt a strange hitch in her chest. "And then you...did get to know each other?"

His gaze was steady. "Just friends, Delia. Nothing more."

"I wasn't asking—"

"Weren't you?"

She exhaled. "Maybe." She shook her head. "I'm so bad at this."

He frowned. "At what?"

She chewed the inside of her cheek. "You know. Important stuff."

He threaded his fingers through hers. "I don't think you're doing so bad. What're your instincts telling you?"

"I wasted two years angling for a guy who had *no* interest in me whatsoever. Does that sound like someone with good instincts?"

"Unless you're still in love with him, I'd say it might just be my good fortune."

"I don't think I was ever in love with him. Which is also proof that I'm not good with the important—" He was kissing her palm. She moistened her lips. "Do you want to go with me to a party in a couple of weeks?"

He smiled slightly. "What kind of party?"

"The worst. One of my grandmother's *soirees.*" She drew the word out.

His smile widened. "Will it be in the *conservatory*?"

She felt a bubble of laughter. "With Vivian, who knows? It's just family so it's pretty much a guarantee it won't be dull."

"How can I resist that?" He kissed her knuckles. "Are you going to finish the pizza or are we taking it with us for breakfast?"

Something inside her chest swooped then rose up again. "I don't have a toothbrush with me," she said huskily.

"Pretty sure we can figure something out." He flagged down their server and in short order they'd left the restaurant.

In his upstairs apartment once more, Delia used the bathroom and then hurriedly straightened the bedding that they'd left in a tangle. It was difficult not feeling as nervous as a schoolgirl because, for all her supposed experience, she'd never once spent an entire night with a man.

If she were honest, she was a shaking mess inside.

She left the bedroom and watched him moving around in the kitchen area, straightening the few pieces of mail sitting on the table and rinsing the few mugs in the sink before sticking them in the dishwasher and starting it. Then he hung up his coat on a peg and draped hers over the back of one of the chairs.

She realized she was smiling.

He noticed. "What?"

"Have you always been this tidy?"

He turned off the kitchen light, which left only the light from the bedroom seeping in. "Not always. But then, for a long time, it was the only thing I could control. And now the habit's stuck."

She forgot about her nerves and slipped into his arms. "There are worse habits. I'm guilty of most of them, no doubt." She tucked her head against his chest in a spot that seemed uniquely perfect. She could feel his breath. Hear his heartbeat. "Do you see your brothers often? Your mom?"

"Couple times a year." She felt his lips brush her temple. "Holidays. Often enough."

"I saw my mom just yesterday," she murmured. "And everywhere I turn I'm running into family."

"Do you need to let someone know where you are?"

Did she? "I suppose I should let Montrose know." She pulled away and found her phone in her coat pocket. She turned it so he could see the display. "Six hundred and ninety." She dialed Montrose's extension at the mansion. "That's how many people have made submissions on that website."

Montrose didn't answer, which was fine with her. She left a message that she wouldn't be returning to the mansion that night and she would speak with her grandmother at some point tomorrow.

As soon as she ended the call, six hundred and ninety became six hundred and ninety-one.

"You *can* turn off cell phones," he pointed out.

"Do you turn off yours?"

He spread his hands. "I own a small business, sweetheart. I don't work and my people don't get paid."

She didn't own anything except the clothes in her

closet and her car still parked in front of the garage. And once Vivian and Squire realized the error of their ways, she wouldn't even have a job. It was a good thing she lived at the mansion rent-free. "Yes, but your business closes at five. Sign on the door says so."

"What time was it when I was hookin' up your car to a winch?"

"Okay, so I can probably turn mine off more easily than you can yours. But," she waggled the phone in her hand, "I have two ragingly pregnant cousins who could go into labor at any moment." She set the phone on the table. "Though five days from now between the hours of noon and midnight would be okay, too."

"Oddly specific."

She chuckled and told him about the baby pool as she moved around the perimeter of the living area, touching this, looking more closely at that. "Did you always want to be a mechanic?"

"I wanted to be a farmer. Like my dad."

She tried to imagine him riding a tractor in a field somewhere. "But you didn't stay in Idaho?"

"No land left to farm." His eyes looked far away. "We tried to keep up the payments but—" He shook his head. "Bank took back the land. Then the county decided to get in our business and help by separating my brothers and me into foster homes while Mom tried to dry out. For a while there, the only time I saw my brothers was at school. But even then, we weren't all at the same school at the same time. Not with ten years between Adair and Dev."

"Did you get to go back to your mom?"

"Eventually." He leaned against the back of the couch. "Was the only thing we all wanted. To go home. None of us were smart enough to be model children. We didn't exactly help the situation. Some of the stupid stuff we pulled…" He shook his head. "I always had a knack for dismantling things."

"What do you mean?"

"Taking things apart. Like…other people's cars."

"I still don't understand."

"I jacked car parts."

"Oh." Realization hit. "Seriously?" Then she stiffened. "You don't still—"

He laughed softly, shaking his head. "Not since I was fifteen," he assured her. "I was in high school. Had an auto shop teacher who didn't bust me when he could have. Instead he kept on me until I knew as much about putting things together as I did about taking them apart. Made sure I got into a trade school. Got certified." He lifted his arms. "All led to here."

"Never wanted to go to college?"

He shook his head. "Wasn't my path."

"Nor mine," she murmured. "Your mom got sober, though." He'd told her that earlier. "How long has it been?"

"Twenty-two months." He must have read her shock. "The time before that was six years. Conquering it takes courage. Vigilance. Sometimes she runs out of both. She does the best she can."

"I don't know if all kids in your situation would be so accepting. I don't know if I would be," she admitted.

He didn't answer. Just turned on the television. But the picture didn't come on. Instead, music came through the speakers. Piano music, specifically.

Low. Slow.

And achingly romantic.

He held out his hand.

She put her hand in his and he slowly reeled her in.

That sensation inside of swooping and soaring returned and no amount of willpower was going to make it stop. "Nice move, cowboy," she tried, but the delivery was miserable. Husky. Shaky.

"Years of practice," he murmured and lifted her hand, twirling her gently.

"I think I'm jealous," she whispered.

"Watching my parents dance." His voice seemed to drop an octave. He pulled her in close again. "Every night after my dad came in from working all day in the field, he'd dance with my mom." Another slow twirl. Like something out of a dream. "Until I started school, I thought it was what everybody's mom and dad did before you sat down to supper each night." He waited a beat. "He danced with her every night until the day he died."

Delia's eyes were damp. She didn't know if he was breaking her heart or putting it together. "They must have loved each other very much."

He didn't answer. Just continued slowly revolving with her until the music finally stopped.

Then he drew her into the bedroom once more and she slept the whole night through in his arms.

Chapter Fifteen

Nobody won the baby pool that night. Or the next.

When Delia went to Gold Creek on Monday morning to meet Charmaine for her first day as manager, both of her cousins had yet to pop out a baby.

She'd spent Saturday morning at the mansion since Mac's shop was open on Saturday mornings. By some miracle, she'd missed both Vivian and Stewart. She hadn't been so lucky where Montrose was concerned. He'd seemed to expect an explanation of where she'd spent her time.

She'd reminded him that she was well over twenty-one and walked out of the house again, but this time with an oversized purse on her shoulder.

In it, she'd stuffed a change of clothes. Her toothbrush.

And some of that languishing lingerie.

As much as she would have preferred to stay with Mac, she'd gone back to the mansion Sunday evening. Sitting through dinner while Stewart droned on about the latest content for the website had been a lot more tolerable since she'd still been floating on air after the hours spent with Mac. Vivian had turned in early. She was clearly still harboring the notion that Stewart and Delia were getting closer.

Even though Delia had wanted to foster that notion, she'd still felt guilty about it when she headed to the west wing for the night. But when she'd gone to set the record straight the next morning, Vivian was closed in her office on a phone call with Stewart Senior.

Knowing Charmaine would be waiting, she'd left vowing to herself that she'd talk to Vivian as soon as she could.

It had snowed again overnight, but when she turned into the parking lot at Gold Creek, it—like Main Street—had already been plowed. Likewise with Mac's parking area. The pile of snow on the side of his garage was higher than ever and all his bays were open and occupied.

She parked behind the rec center near the dumpsters and storage shed where Charmaine was already waiting. The second she spotted Delia, she climbed out of her car.

Delia grabbed the box of things she'd collected from her office at the mansion and joined her. "Morning." She punched in the security code to the main building and pulled open the door. "Have a good weekend?"

"I did." Charmaine followed her inside. "Maybe not as good as you," she qualified with a grin. "Mac mentioned your name two or twenty times when he came over to plow the parking lot."

"*He* did that?"

"Finished just a few minutes before you got here. Town of Weaver only does the public buildings and main thoroughfares. They'll do a sweep through the residential areas but only once a week. So if they've already plowed after one snow and more falls afterward, you're stuck for the rest of that week."

"I forget how spoiled I'm getting at my grandmother's," Delia admitted. She flipped on a row of switches and light flickered throughout the building. "The drive in and out of the mansion is always meticulously clear. Winter. Summer. Anytime in between."

"I can only dream. I have to shovel my way out of my garage way too often. No Stewart?"

"Not today. He's drafting boilerplate funding agreements for my grandmother's foundation." Privately, she thought he would have come up with anything if it meant avoiding the rec center, knowing their first day would be spent getting the place in order.

"How's that going, anyway? *WEAVERFUNDS?*" Charmaine was pulling off her coat, her expression bright and curious as she looked around.

"Slower than things around here." If one didn't

count the rising number of inquiries at the website. The list was now at eight hundred and three. "So. Manager Macdonald." She spread her arms. "What do you want to tackle first?"

Charmaine lifted her hands. "Am I going to start things off wrong if I admit this all looks more overwhelming than I expected? Especially when we're supposed to open in just a week?"

Delia felt the same way. The remodeling had taken months. And though the construction workers were gone, taking their equipment with them, there was still a lot of mess left behind. "How about we both pick out our offices," she suggested. "And then we'll just start a list. Work our way down."

Charmaine chose the only office that was in the front of the building. "This way I can see people as they're coming and going."

Delia, on the other hand, chose an office in the very back. Then they walked through the building together making their list. It was quickly apparent that they needed some serious cleaning supplies. So they locked up again and went to Shop-World. Twice.

By lunchtime, they'd hauled, mopped, sweated and cursed their way through half of the building.

"I don't know about you," Delia said, "but I need a major pick-me-up before we start on the day care wing."

Charmaine looked a little less worse for wear than Delia felt. "What do you have in mind?"

"Chocolate shake at Ruby's Diner."

Charmaine shook her head ruefully. "I don't know how you can eat like you do and still look like you do."

Delia tucked her tongue in her cheek. "Clean living." She swept her arm at the mess remaining. "That stuff isn't going anywhere."

When they arrived at Ruby's, the diner was as busy as ever. Delia was surprised to see Gloria and Squire Clay sitting together in a corner booth. Considering the sideways looks they were getting from the other patrons, she wasn't the only one who was surprised.

She hoped it meant that their troubled waters were smoothing out, but it didn't exactly look auspicious with the way they were squared off on opposite sides of the table.

Rather than wait for a table or booth to themselves, she and Charmaine headed straight for the counter where three seats were available. The specials were written on a board on the wall and when the waitress Tina asked if they wanted menus, they both shook their heads. Charmaine ordered a quinoa salad and Delia ordered a double-cheeseburger and shake.

"Hey." She recognized the look on Charmaine's face. "For some of us it's just as hard to keep weight on."

"I wouldn't mind a month or two of the problem," Charmaine said dryly.

The noise level in the diner was plenty high but there was no way to miss the clatter of dishes when it rang out. Delia looked over to see Gloria striding out of the diner. Her temper was obvious in the way she slammed open the door and left.

"Oh dear," Tina murmured behind the counter.

Squire remained in the booth, seeming impervious to the spaghetti splattered across his chest.

A waitress Delia didn't know was crouching around the floor, picking up the plate that Gloria must have thrown at him. After a moment Squire slid out of the booth, too.

He walked toward the counter. His demeanor dared anyone to comment as he paid Tina, who had quickly scooted over to the cash register. "Sorry for the mess." His quiet voice was perfectly audible in the shocked silence.

Tina ducked her chin. She looked like she might cry. "Don't worry about it, Squire."

He waved off the change she tried to hand him and left.

The second he did, voices erupted.

"Ohmigod, did you *see* that?"

"If someone threw food at me like that?"

"D'you s'pose she'll get half the Double-C? I heard it's worth millions—"

Delia and Charmaine looked at each other and slowly turned back around to face the counter.

"Wow," Charmaine murmured. "I've seen some things as a bartender but never anything quite like that."

Delia hadn't seen anything quite like that, either.

And it wasn't the spaghetti. It was the look in the old man's eyes.

The look of defeat.

Her phone pinged and she automatically glanced at it. Eight hundred and nineteen.

She turned it facedown and wished she hadn't ordered the double cheeseburger. She hardly felt hungry anymore.

Charmaine wasn't similarly affected.

Which was good in a way.

She pulled out the folder she'd brought with her and set it on the counter between them. "These are the notes I made on the job applications Stewart gave me. I wanted to run a few ideas by you about some of the job descriptions Marty came up with."

By the time Charmaine was finished, Delia had sucked half her way through her thick milkshake and gotten her mind off Squire and back onto Gold Creek. Time was essential at this point and since she already knew so many of the job applicants personally, they both agreed that Charmaine should just hire them straight off if their interviews went well.

Tina left the check and Delia reached for it. "On me today," she told Charmaine.

"I'm not going to argue. Pay cut and all that," Charmaine said with a wink. She excused herself to visit the restroom while Delia paid the tab.

The spaghetti mess in the corner was long cleared away and Delia glanced around at the diners who'd all seemed to return to normal, the excitement seemingly forgotten.

Her phone pinged and she glanced at it again.

Fancy another shower?

She smiled and tried to think of a clever response.

"I know that sort of smile," Charmaine said, returning just then.

She felt a little flushed as she hit *Send* on her painfully unimaginative yes!! and turned the phone facedown on the counter. "I don't know what you mean." She picked up her milkshake and sucked hard on the straw. The shake had melted down a lot and shot up the straw hard enough to make her cough.

Charmaine's grin deepened. "Mac doesn't go around, ah, snowplowing for just anybody."

Delia pressed her napkin to her mouth, coughing harder than ever.

Charmaine slapped her on the back and pushed her glass of water toward her. She was laughing silently.

They returned to the rec center. The garage bays across the street were still open and the tow truck was gone. Delia had met Mac's two apprentices and she could see one of them tossing an old tire onto the pile in a trailer.

Knowing what pleasures awaited later with Mac, Delia started in on the preschool room with renewed vigor.

Elsewhere in the building, Charmaine had turned on a radio. Delia could hear her singing along to the music.

They had to take another break when two delivery trucks arrived.

"You're a lot more organized at this than I am," Delia admitted ruefully. Everything that Marty had ordered from alphabet blocks to play xylophones had been dumped haphazardly inside the lobby right alongside office furniture, sports equipment and fitness machines. "It wouldn't occur to me to categorize everything before even trying to move stuff to where it belongs." They were using color-coded labels that Charmaine had run across the street to buy at the convenience store.

"Will make it easier in the end," Charmaine assured. "We're going to have to call in some muscle for the big stuff. Ain't no way you and I can move it all on our own." She finished cutting away the cardboard from around a narrow filing cabinet. "But there are a few things we can manage. So we're not tripping over stuff out here and we can at least get people through the front door. We have—" she glanced at her watch "—just over an hour before Maia comes in." She tossed the cardboard onto the growing pile of shrink wrap and other packing materials. "You game?"

They moved the filing cabinet and two others just like it to the offices they'd chosen earlier. They even succeeded in pushing the unassembled desks to their prospective homes.

Exhausted, they took another break. This time they sat on a bench next to the swimming pool.

"Will it be filled by the grand opening?"

"It better be. We're going to want to show it off."

Delia rotated her sore feet. "I wish it was filled now. I'd fall in fully dressed at this point."

"I can't wait to get Ethan and Carmela signed up for lessons."

"They don't swim?"

"Not well," Charmaine admitted. "They don't have a lot of opportunity to swim anywhere." She rubbed her shoulder. "Ethan's at the point where he'd rather not participate at all than let on he's not an expert. I'm hoping Mac'll convince him. He's done so much already."

Delia felt her nerves tighten in a way that had nothing to do with their hours of grunt work. She was still as much in the dark about why Charmaine's kids "spent Tuesdays" with Mac as ever.

Charmaine pushed off the bench and went over to a stack of leftover ceramic tile. She picked up one of the shiny blue squares. "Does this stuff get returned for credit or something?"

"I don't think so. I'd have to ask Nick Ventura. He's the one who was in charge of all that stuff." She felt her brain throbbing a little. "So…sounds like Mac and your kids are pretty close."

"Thank God." Charmaine wandered down the length of the pool. Her voice echoed a little in the space. "He tell you about Ethan breaking into his garage?"

"He mentioned it," she said casually.

"I thought I'd lose my mind. My ex-husband was on another one of his rants to take custody away from me—that's what we were at the court for last week, *again*. He's always claiming I'm not providing a proper environment blah-blah-blah." She rolled her eyes. "As if *he* and his revolving door of skanks would be better. Anyway, so a couple years ago, I get a call from Mac that he'd caught my formerly sweet baby boy trying to climb out the window with a couple catalytic converters. Ethan had learned from somewhere that they contain platinum and *brilliantly* thought he was going to get rich." She shook her head. "I could've strangled him."

"What happened?"

"Mac said he had to work off the cost of the broken window and the two parts or he was going to turn him in. Naturally Ethan tried arguing that he hadn't gotten *away* with the converters so why should that be a factor. Honestly, at the time I didn't necessarily disagree. But he needed a big-time course correction or Eddie really was going to have a leg to stand on in our custody dispute. And that's how Tuesdays with Mac evolved."

She retraced her steps around the perimeter of the pool. "Ethan didn't even notice when he'd worked off his sentence. Mac had gotten him that hooked on cars. Then Carmela got jealous about Ethan getting to learn that sort of thing, and Mac of course said bring her along." She smiled. "Last time I needed an oil change, *she* did it."

"Good for her." Delia's chest had gotten tight. Mac was doing for Ethan what his former teacher had done for him and providing a young girl with independent skills along the way.

"And then," Charmaine was on a roll, "the sheriff's department got wind of what Mac had done with Ethan and asked if he'd be willing to take another wannabe miscreant under his wing. And Mac—he's such a softy. He had twelve kids coming to his garage at one point. You met Toby Rutledge yet? He was one of Mac's kids before he graduated high school. I think Carmela said they were back down to nine again. Even when they no longer *have* to go, most of them end up wanting to stick around, same way Ethan did. You," she pointed at Delia with the tile in her hand, "have got a good one there, girlfriend."

"How come the two of you—"

"—oh, hell no." Charmaine shook her head vehemently. "He's a good-looking man for sure. But not my type at all."

"Which is?" She was genuinely curious.

"Considering my history?" Charmaine rolled her eyes. "Slick good-for-nothings." She set the tile back on the stack. "Suppose we should get back to it." They'd spent half the afternoon dealing with the deliveries and the first of the appointments she'd scheduled was due to arrive soon. "Every minute spent is a minute closer to the grand opening."

"You're totally right, there." Delia heaved herself to her feet. The effort had her thinking of Hayley and Ali. "While you're taking care of interviews, I need to make a few calls myself. I'll see if I can't round up some muscle while I'm at it."

Charmaine headed for her office and Delia headed to hers. She sat on the floor and pulled out her cell phone. No babies. *WEAVERFUNDS* submissions now at eight-eighty. She called Stewart to check on his progress. He'd finished the boilerplate agreements.

"We're getting close to the point where we're going to need to be able to say, specifically, what areas the foundation is funding," he warned. "It's even more important than the name."

She rubbed a bruise on her arm that she hadn't noticed. She thought about Squire and Gloria. "Have you seen Vivian today?"

"In passing."

She sighed. "Right now, we have to get the rec center open. Charmaine hopes to have a few new hires today."

"Provisional hires," he reminded. "Nothing's permanent until they've cleared background checks."

"I remember." She'd already made sure Charmaine's signed form was among the paperwork she'd given Delia. She just needed to drop it off at the sheriff's department. Most of the other forms would go to Emily Clay for payroll purposes.

They ended the call and even though she would have liked to stretch right out on the floor, she made herself get up and fill the mop bucket yet again because the whole childcare wing was still waiting to be mopped.

She was still at it when Charmaine found her. "I'm heading out for the day." She had a stack of familiar looking packets with her. "Four hires," she said with a broad smile. "Plus the Forrest boys, that's six already. More people coming in tomorrow starting at ten."

"That's great, Charmaine."

"Are you going to stay?"

"For a little while." She looked at the streaky floor around her. "I cannot face coming in tomorrow thinking I've got to mop another inch of floor. You go ahead. Have a good evening at home with your kids."

Beaming, the other woman left.

Delia wiped her arm across her forehead and slopped the mop over the floor again. She was on the last quarter of the large preschool classroom when she heard footsteps behind her. "What'd you forget?" She looked over her shoulder.

Mac stood there.

Her heart seemed to skip a beat. He wore jeans and a flannel shirt that made his eyes look even bluer. "What're you doing here?"

He held up a cardboard box. "As a picnic basket it doesn't look like much—" he tilted it slightly so she could see inside "—but it does the job. And I figured you'd be starving by now."

She lifted the checkered blanket that was folded on top. Beneath was a bucket of takeout chicken, a bottle of wine, a bottle of soda and a package of store-bought cookies.

"Cookies aren't quite Montrose-quality," he said.

Feeling like she just might burst, she pushed her fingers through his hair and tugged his head down. "I think they look perfect."

She was beginning to think he was perfect, too.

Chapter Sixteen

The next afternoon, Mac, along with his apprentices and his Tuesday troop, came across the street and helped move color-coded items to color-coded places.

Charmaine continued with interviews and Delia followed Mac around as he assembled desks, chairs and storage shelves and she ran back and forth to the dumpsters in the back of their building disposing of more packing materials. She pored over instructions for elliptical machines and treadmills and weight systems that Mac was able to comprehend in a glance and tried to convince him that his Tuesday program with Ethan and the others was worth turning into something more official.

"If you established a nonprofit program, you could get funding," she said.

"And I'd have to deal with a lot of red-tape, too," he countered. "Hand me that screwdriver, would you? The one with the red handle."

"Then you *have* thought about it?"

"Yeah, and I thought about what outside funding would mean for being able to spend more afternoons with more kids who need some direction." He pointed at the toolbox. "Red handle. I'm not a do-gooder, Delia. I'm a mechanic."

"You're a whole lot more than that," she insisted. "Promise me you'll at least think about it?"

He exhaled noisily. "If I promise, will you finally hand me that screwdriver?"

She smiled and handed it to him.

They didn't share a picnic on a checkered blanket in the preschool classroom this time, but it had still been a nearly perfect day. Particularly when they went back across the street to his apartment and Mac pulled her into the shower...

By Wednesday night, Charmaine had amazingly managed to fill all the most critical job positions. She was on a roll. "Judge dismissed Eddie's latest case today," she told Delia. "My attorney says my getting this job was what pushed it over the top. I'm taking the kids to Colbys to celebrate. Want to come?"

Delia was happy for her. "I can't do dinner, though. I've told my grandmother I'll be dining with her."

"Another time, then." Judging by Charmaine's expression, nothing was going to dim her elation.

Delia filled in Vivian about the rec center's progress over dinner that evening. "Charmaine's been amazing."

"She sounds like a very hard worker." Vivian held out her wineglass for Montrose to refill and peered at Delia. "Sounds like you've been quite industrious yourself the last few days, as well."

"There's been a lot to do at Gold Creek." Delia toyed with her fork. Montrose's coq au vin was impeccable as usual, but she knew she would have preferred bucket chicken with Mac ten times out of ten.

When she'd told him she wanted to check on Vivian, he'd encouraged her to go. He and Grant were picking up a load of appliances from a dealer in Braden who was going out of business anyway. Mac had a shelter in mind that would be able to use everything.

"Besides," he'd nipped her lower lip, "I know you miss that big bathtub in your big bathroom."

"You *could* come and join me later." She'd nipped his lip in return. "Have never tested it, but I'm pretty sure the tub'll hold two…"

"Are you going to just stare through me, Delia, or tell me what's on your mind?"

Vivian's voice cut into her reverie.

Delia set down her fork and folded her hands in her lap. "Where *is* Stewart tonight, anyway?" It was just the two of them sitting at one end of the dining room table.

"He left for Pittsburgh early this morning," Vivian said.

"He didn't tell me."

"Well, dear. Is there any reason why he should? You're sleeping with someone else."

Delia flushed a little.

Her grandmother gave her another over-the-glasses look. "You might have just told me," she chided.

"I *was* going to." Delia reached for her wine. "That's one of the reasons why I'm here this evening." She just hadn't expected to have the opportunity over dinner when Stewart was always there.

"And the other reasons?"

"Is it impossible to think I might miss seeing you every day?"

Vivian gave her a dry look. "Impossible? No. Unlikely perhaps."

She wasn't going to share the fact that her cousins checked in routinely with her regarding their grandmother's well-being. "I wanted to ask about the foundation," she said instead.

It wasn't untrue.

"What about it?"

Delia took a sip of her wine. Set the glass down precisely. "Do you really think I'm capable of administering it?"

Vivian's eyes narrowed slightly. "I've said so, haven't I? If anyone has doubted your capability, it's been you."

She nodded. It was true. "And if I ask you a question, an important question, in all seriousness. Will you answer?"

Vivian toyed with the giant diamond on her ring

finger for so long that Delia decided her grandmother wasn't going to even answer *that* question. She exhaled. "Is Stewart coming back?" He was still supposed to be advising her, wasn't he?

"*That* is your important question?"

Delia's lips tightened. "You know very well that it isn't."

"Yes, he will be returning." Vivian focused on her coq au vin. "He's handling a few matters for me."

Her grandmother was being no more cryptic than she usually was.

"Why are you and Squire at such a stalemate over the foundation's name and purpose?"

Vivian's fork paused midair. She slowly set it down again. "We don't entirely disagree on the purpose." She picked up her napkin and dabbed her lips. "He wants to strictly fund projects focused on women's and children's health."

Delia absorbed that. She didn't really have any preconceived notions about the foundation, but she was somewhat surprised anyway. "I guess that makes sense. He was one of the driving forces behind the hospital being built." Which had occurred long before Vivian came to Wyoming and announced her existence to her grandchildren. "But you want to focus on something else instead? Education?" It was—no pun intended—an educated guess, since Arthur had been a schoolteacher.

"It isn't that I don't want to fund what Squire wants. It's that I don't want to *only* fund what he wants. As usual, the man is shortsighted. Can't see beyond the tip of his nose. There's no earthly reason why we should limit the resources we have to share in that way. And yes, education would be one of my choices. Obviously. Arts and culture." She exhaled softly. "Not *just* what he wants."

"Okay. That's fair. Does he think there won't be enough funds to make a real impact if your focus is too broad? A million dollars is a lot of money to give away every year but not if we're divvying it up to every person or organization that sticks out their hand. Or maybe he's worried about kicking in his ten mil. I know you have scads of money, Vivvie, but—"

"—he's contributing two." Vivian suddenly began studying her rings again. "Million. The rest is coming from me."

Delia went silent. She could hear the tick of the antique clock on the mantel. "Yet you both have equal say how it's used," she finally said. "That's hardly your usual style, Vivian. I know you're trying to atone for the way you treated his wife. But it was what? Sixty-some years ago? Isn't eighteen million taking it a little far?"

"Sawyer would have approved of any amount," Vivian said. "Frankly, the money is immaterial."

"Only someone with as much of it as you have could get away with a statement like that. So, aside from the idea of funding more types of things than he wants, why can't you agree on the name of the foundation?" She watched Montrose as he topped off Vivian's wine, ignored *her* and left the room once again.

Troll.

"Squire insists the foundation be named only after her," Vivian finally said. "The Sarah Benedict Foundation. That was her family name. I would agree to the Templeton-Clay Foundation. Or even Clay-Templeton. But no. Even after I'm willing to put a fortune into his idea, he's adamant. Because still, despite every way I've tried to make up for the past, he wants to make sure *I* never forget the callous way I treated his beloved wife."

Delia pressed her fingertips to her eyes. She wished she'd never asked. "I'm sorry."

"Don't be," Vivian said wearily.

"And my part in this weird plot? Did he pick the most irresponsible grandchild you have and stick you with me?"

"You were the one person we *could* agree upon."

"Why?"

"Because you don't care about the money. And I don't mean that you're careless about the money. I mean that you aren't swayed by it. You don't love it. You certainly haven't spurned it like your father and uncle. And lastly—I'm sorry if it hurts—but you're the one who is *available*."

"You mean I can't find a *man*?"

"Delia. Honestly." As if she couldn't bear to sit at the table with her, Vivian rose and began pacing. "I mean that you haven't found your passion in life. Once you do, then you'll pursue it with all the verve you bring to everything that matters to you. We don't intend to shackle you to the foundation for the rest of your days!"

She clutched the long loops of pearls around her neck and sat back down. "So now you know the entire story. Not even partnering a small fortune with that old rancher will soften his hide. If you want to unsaddle yourself from the whole matter, say so now. It'll be one more thing I can have Stewart take care of while he's away."

"Not sure I like the visual of being saddled," Delia muttered, "but I'm not quitting." She picked up her fork and jabbed a mushroom but she couldn't make herself eat it.

"Anyway, you do have a man," Vivian said after a moment.

"What?"

"You said you can't find a—"

"I remember."

"Are you serious about him?"

She huffed and tossed back a quarter of the contents of her wineglass.

"Don't get dramatic with me, dear."

Delia narrowed her eyes. "Since all the cards are on the table…why didn't you ever ask if things were serious where *Nick* was concerned?"

"Because I knew it wasn't."

"Wish somebody had told *me*," Delia groused, if only for the sake of grousing. What she felt for Mac was so, so much more…

Vivian was still waiting for an answer to her question, one eyebrow raised slightly. Delia knew from experience the woman could wait like that indefinitely when she wanted.

"I don't *know*! Okay? Can you ever know if something's serious? What happens if you think it's serious and after two, three, thirty years, you realize you were wrong? *You* were married four times—"

"And widowed." Vivian pulled off her glasses and sat back slightly in her chair. "Four times. That doesn't mean I am unaware that sometimes, a relationship simply runs its course. It's meant to be for only a finite amount of time. But sometimes—" Her expression turned far away. "Sometimes it's meant for infinity."

Delia chest felt oddly tight. "Arthur was your infinity."

"Not was, Delia. *Is*." Vivian's lips curved in a bittersweet smile. "I loved Sawyer. And I still believe that he loved me right up until he died, despite what your father and Carter think. But I was so young and so caught up in appearances. In what I believed our position in society was supposed to be. Even aside from him discovering he had an illegitimate sister and wanting to bring her into the family fold, our marriage was far from perfect. I thought it was my sacred duty to show the world that it was. Perfect wife. Home. Children." She sighed. "So much foolishly wasted effort on appearances and look at where it has led me."

"What about Theodore and Magnus?"

"They were useful at the time."

Delia winced. "I know you can be cold—"

"Make no mistake, darling. Marrying Vivian Archer Templeton was equally useful to them." Her lips twisted. "If not more so. But once again, you didn't listen well. I didn't ask if matters were serious between you and Macnair."

"Naturally," she muttered. Not only did her grandmother know who Mac was, but she knew who he *was*. Nobody called Mac by his full name. Not even his own mother. He'd told her that. "What'd you do? Have him investigated?" Vivian had been known to do it before when it came to people her other grandchildren got involved with.

Delia had just always thought she was exempt from that.

"What I *asked* you—" exasperation was creeping back into her grandmother's tone "—was if *you* were serious. Do you have real feelings for Mac—"

"I'm sorry," Montrose interrupted. He'd materialized next to Vivian. "You have a visitor. Shall I put him in the library?"

"For pity's sake, Montrose." Annoyance was a red flag on Vivian's cheeks. "You order this entire household around three hundred and sixty-five days of the year. Can't you deal with this while I'm *trying* to have a conversation with my granddaughter?"

He sniffed imperiously. "May I remind you that I am a *chef*?"

Delia had to cover her snort with a cough.

"If you want a *bouncer*—" he sounded even haughtier "—call on Bubba Bumble. I am sure he throws people around routinely." He snatched up the wine decanter and stomped back through the connecting door to the kitchen.

"I've fired you nine times, Montrose," Vivian called heatedly after him. "Would you like a tenth?"

"Well." The voice at the main doorway of the room drew Delia and Vivian's attention.

Squire Clay stood there. His cowboy hat was on his head, his gnarled walking stick in his hand. Didn't matter what age he was. Or that his wife had recently tossed spaghetti on him in front of an entire diner full of people. He still stood tall and unyielding.

"I see you're still staying true to form, Vivian."

Vivian tossed up her hands. "Oh, why not. My home has become a circus."

Delia stood and walked around her, leaning down toward her ear. "Dial down *your* drama, Grandmother," she said softly. "That man doesn't need it from you. Not today."

Vivian tossed her head but said nothing. She curled her beringed fingers and narrowed her eyes.

Delia crossed the room. She stopped next to Squire. "If you need anything, I won't be far."

Then she moved past him through the doorway. She looked back, giving Vivian a warning look.

Whether or not her grandmother saw it, though, was anybody's guess.

Because Squire Clay reached out and quietly closed the door in Delia's face.

Gnawing the inside of her cheek, she went into the kitchen. She sat down across from Montrose at the stainless-steel island. He'd poured a glass of wine from the decanter for himself. "What do you think is going on between them?" she asked.

"I wouldn't know."

"I'm worried."

He hooked another glass from the drawer where they were stored. He set it on the island and filled it from the decanter. Then he nudged the glass toward her. "So am I."

She sighed and took a sip.

He was listening as hard as she was for some snippet from the dining room. It wasn't entirely impossible to eavesdrop.

But there was nothing.

"The coq au vin was delicious," she eventually said.

He topped off his wine and gave her a heavy-lidded look. "Of course it was."

She tipped her glass in acknowledgment.

Good old Montrose.

"Maybe they'll just change their minds." Mac squeezed the large natural sponge in his hand and warm water cascaded over Delia's arms. If he didn't try stretching out his legs, the bathtub in her en suite had plenty of room for two.

It was nearing midnight.

Whatever had been said between Squire and Vivian was still a mystery.

He had left hours ago, and she had retreated to the conservatory.

For the first time Delia could remember, her grandmother had closed the glass doors.

Message clear.

Do not disturb.

When Mac had arrived a little after ten, Montrose had let him in and directed him to the west wing where Delia had been waiting.

In the tub. Full of bubbles. Naked.

Mac's knees were well above the bubble-line, and she slowly swished her hands, watching the velvety suds cling to his thighs. "Change their minds? Dissolve the foundation before it's even done anything?" She shook her head. "After what Vivian said earlier, I think they've both got their heels dug in so far they wouldn't even know how to pull them out if they tried."

"What about you? Are you still willing to be the third wheel in all this?"

"She said Stewart could take care of it…" Delia rubbed the back of her head against Mac's chest. "I don't know."

"Sure you weren't ever interested in him?"

The question surprised her so much she splashed water over the side of the tub sitting up to look at him. His lashes were at half-mast. "In Stewart?"

"I don't mean Squire," he said dryly. "So? Were you?"

"Interested isn't the right word."

He lifted the sponge again and water coursed over her shoulder. He seemed to be focused on the water's progress downward over her breast, trailing bubbles in its wake. "What is?"

"Curious, I think." She inhaled deeply, just for the pleasure of knowing that what he saw pleased him, too. "It lasted about all of a minute." She flattened her palms on his knees and slowly ran them over his thighs beneath the water.

His lids lowered a fraction, leaving little more than a slit of blue. "What happens if they *do* dissolve the foundation? Leaves you out of a job, doesn't it?" He squeezed the sponge again.

"I suppose it does." She leaned closer until her rigid nipples barely brushed the bubbles clinging to his chest. She was already melting inside in anticipation.

"Will you go back to being Vivian's assistant?"

"I don't know." Her hands slid another inch along his thighs. Then two. "Maybe I could learn auto repair." She closed her hand around him.

He inhaled deeply. The corners of his lips quirked ever so slightly. "You do have a certain touch."

She closed the distance and rubbed her lips lightly against his. "Woman learns a few things in her life."

She felt his smile against her mouth. "Long as it wasn't in sixth grade with Teddy Bodecker."

"Tommy Bodecker."

"Whatever." He suddenly jackknifed upward, scooping her along with him.

Water sloshed wildly, dousing the three candles she'd lit for romantic ambience on the marble towel ledge. He stepped out of the tub and carried her into her bedroom.

She was thrilled.

And she was seriously, inescapably in love.

With typical disregard for the water streaming down their limbs, he settled her gently on the bed but when she held out her arms for him to join her, he hesitated.

"What?"

He picked her phone up from the nightstand and turned the display toward her. There was a text.

noon-to-midnight alert. ali at hospital.

Delia pushed Mac aside and darted into the bathroom to grab towels. She pitched one at him as she hurriedly dragged the other over her body. Then she snatched up the jeans she'd left lying in a heap on the floor after he'd texted that he was on his way to the mansion.

"Hurry up," she said when he just stood there. Aroused. Holding the towel and watching her as if he couldn't quite believe it.

"Words a man sometimes wants to hear, sometimes not so much." He tossed the towel around his neck. "What's the rush? Babies take more than five minutes to arrive."

"*Five* minutes?" She gave up trying to work the denim past her damp calves and snatched up the towel again. "As if. Since when do you take so little time?" The man had a seemingly inexhaustible stamina, never letting go until he'd driven her again and again beyond the edge of sanity.

He grabbed the towel from her and tossed her onto the bed. He followed her down, sinking into her with breathtaking purpose. "Time me if you have to," he said against her lips.

She didn't have to.

Twenty minutes later, they were striding through the entrance of the hospital.

"Ten to drive." Mac's voice was low as he followed her toward the information desk where a woman sat typing at a computer. "Five to dress."

She swatted the air as if he were a fly.

"Five to—" He smiled when she shot him a quelling look. "Twice," he finished.

And she felt like she was still vibrating as a result.

It had been an evening of too many lows and highs. And right then, she just wanted to know if Ali'd had the baby yet. It was almost midnight.

Delia didn't care about her grandmother's money. She *did* care about winning the baby pool. It wasn't often she got to lord it over her family members.

She reached the information desk. "We're here for Ali Cooper. She's having a baby."

The volunteer turned away from the computer and Delia blinked with surprise. Gloria Clay's smile was friendly as she handed them two visitor badges. "They're up in labor and delivery. You can go on up."

Chapter Seventeen

"I still can't believe they sent me home from the hospital last night," Ali complained. She jammed a thumbtack through the end of a twist of red-and-white streamers and stuck it into the wall.

"You weren't in labor." Meredith let the crepe paper streamers unwind from the spools, twisting them together as she went. With her dark curly hair sweeping the small of her back and her jeans fraying at her knees, she looked more like Ali's sister than her mother. "Should they have kept you at the hospital anyway?"

Ali still looked disgruntled. "It's not like this is my first time at the rodeo. *Felt* like I was having contractions."

"I'm sure it did," Meredith soothed.

They were decorating the lobby at the rec center in preparation for the grand opening, still four days away.

"Not to sound too selfish but I would've appreciated you popping out that baby, too," Delia said. She was sitting on the floor with Ali's three-year-old pushing plastic cars. Not because Meredith and Ali had both decided she was bad at hanging streamers—she was—but because Reid had wanted "Deeya," so Deeya had happily handed over the duty.

"Yeah, you wanted her to have the baby so you could win the baby pool pot," Connor Forrest said. He took the streamer that Meredith pinched together and affixed it high on the wall.

His brother was wheeling a tall cylinder filled with helium into the lobby. "Where do you want me to put this thing?"

"Storage room next to the break room," Charmaine directed. She'd been an impressive whirl of activity the entire day. "We won't blow up the balloons until the morning of the event."

Zach followed her, wheeling the helium tank through the lobby and turning out of sight when they reached the reception desk.

"You *really* placed a bet?" Ali gave Delia an accusatory look.

Connor hooted. "Between you and Grant, you've placed five!"

"Should be a rule that you can't divulge that sort of information," Ali complained.

"You'll have the baby when the baby is ready to

be had," Meredith said calmly, continuing to let out more streamer, twisting and walking slowly. *She* claimed to be an expert in the streamer department, and considering the amount already draped around the rec center, Delia thought the claim had merit. "I've had a dream, so I know."

"Sage wisdom, Mom." Ali's voice turned dry. She winked at Delia. "That why you and Dad didn't answer when Grant called to tell you we were on the way to the hospital?"

"Actually, we were busy."

"Doing what? It was eleven o'clock at night!"

Meredith just lifted her eyebrows slightly.

Ali suddenly made a face. "Oh, *Mom!*"

Meredith didn't bother hiding her smile as she turned back to her task. "You think your generation invented it?"

"Invented what?" Connor asked, looking back and forth like he was watching a tennis match.

"Now look what you started," Ali accused.

Delia chuckled. Connor and Zach were eighteen and more precocious than even *she* had been. "Invented where babies come from in the first place."

"Gross," he muttered, then looked toward Meredith. "No offense."

Meredith just laughed.

Ali waddled over to Delia and her firstborn. She held out her hand. "Come on, Reid baby. There's pizza in the break room. Let's go have a snack."

"I not hungry." He drove his little car over the top of Delia's head. "Wanna stay."

"He's fine," Delia said and rolled down over the toddler, tickling his ribs. He wriggled and squealed and squirmed out from her hold, abandoning his car and reaching for his mother's hand.

Unfortunately, the car was now hopelessly tangled in Delia's hair.

Meredith turned over her streamer duty to work at freeing it.

"There's a sight you don't see every day," Mac observed coming in from the front door.

Delia looked up at him, feeling a bubble of something sweet expand inside her. It was the middle of the afternoon. She hadn't expected to see him until after he'd closed the garage for the day. "Are you talking about the newest in hair fashion or the explosion of cut-out hearts and streamers?"

He leaned over and kissed her nose. "Both." He straightened again. "Can't believe how much you've whipped the place into shape since Monday."

"Charmaine gets all the credit."

"Voila!" Meredith handed Delia the little car. "You're free."

"Thanks." She pushed to her feet and smiled up at Mac. "So, what're you doing here?"

"Have to cancel tonight."

"Oh." She fluttered her lashes. "And I was hoping to practice my wiles on you."

"We already know I'm putty in your hands," he said dryly.

"Let's go back to my office," she told him. She wasn't really needed in the lobby. The boys and

Meredith had the decorating well in hand. "Do you want some pizza? Charmaine picked it up earlier from Ruby's. Not exactly Pizza Bella level yet but that new wood fired oven Tabby put in for Bubba? Betcha he gives them a run for their money soon."

"Already had lunch." Mac walked with her from the lobby down the corridor toward her office. "Filling the pool, I see."

She glanced through the interior windows where the water was slowly creeping up the plaster walls of the indoor pool. "Finally. More of Charmaine's doing. She drove over to the pool guy's house and demanded that he finish what he'd been paid to do." She slid her hand into his. "Everything okay? You look tired." And not just because of a late night involving a fruitless trip to the hospital.

"I fired Toby today."

"Oh, no! I'm so sorry." They turned into her office, and she pulled him down onto the settee that he'd helped her move from her office at Vivian's. She drew her knee up, turning sideways toward him and squeezed his hand. "What happened?" He'd told her about the joy-riding incident on the day before New Year's. "Thought Toby had been toeing the line lately."

"He was. But when I was helping him and Cadell get an engine on the hoist today, he smelled like booze." He shook his head. "Nobody breaks that rule in my shop. You don't come to work if you've been drinking. Too many bad things can happen. So." He exhaled. "He's gone."

She leaned close and pressed her cheek against his for a moment. "What about his mom?"

"She's going to have to figure out another way to make ends meet until Toby finds another job. I feel for the way she lost her husband, but I haven't seen her try to do much to improve her situation. Toby was learning a skill with me. He was never a bad kid. Just doesn't take time to think about consequences." He blew out a noisy breath. "Some rules aren't meant to be broken."

She ran her hand up his forearm, feeling the ridge of his scar. "What does all that have to do with to-night?"

"I have to drive the load of discarded tires over to the recycler in Gillette. It's ready to overflow. I was going to send Toby, but—" He spread his hands.

"You have to drive there today?" Gillette was a two-hour drive, in good weather. "Heard another snowstorm was on its way."

"Storm isn't supposed to hit until tomorrow. It's too late for me to get to the recycler before they close today, but I'll be able to dump the trailer first thing in the morning and head on back. I should beat the storm. Cadell can open the garage, and after that, if you need help around the rec center for the grand opening, I'm at your disposal."

"You'll drive safely?"

He bracketed her face in his palms and kissed her slowly. "What do you think?"

After he left, Delia was still sitting in a blissful haze when Charmaine walked into the office waving a manila envelope. "Last of the...hello? Earth to Delia?"

She focused on the other woman. "What?"

"Boy, you do have it bad." Charmaine fanned the envelope in front of Delia. "Paperwork for the last of the new hires."

"Right." She took the envelope and moved around her desk. She still needed to deal with everyone's forms. "Do you know Toby Rutledge's mom?"

"Amy? Sure. She and Toby have a house on the block behind the Methodist church."

"What does she do for a living?"

"Same thing she's done ever since I've known her. Takes in renters and works part-time at the corner drug. Why?"

She told Charmaine about Mac letting Toby go.

"And he feels bad," Charmaine concluded. "Even though he has no reason to. Told you. Big old softy." She shook her head and left the office again.

Delia wasn't sure she disagreed.

She pulled out the paperwork, glancing through it even though she knew everything would be in order; Charmaine was thorough. She separated out the security clearance forms from all the rest and reached in her drawer to gather the rest of the employee forms. Some positions required a fingerprint check as well as a general background check and she'd already organized them into separate batches. Then she flipped through the payroll-related forms that she needed to deliver to Emily Clay and realized she had missed pulling out Maia's and Charmaine's emergency notification forms.

She removed them from the stack and took them to Charmaine's office. "Forgot a couple emergency forms. I didn't realize Maia and Olivia were related," she commented as she glanced at the form. She'd listed the waitress as her "contact in case of emergency."

"Sisters."

Delia squared up the two pieces of paper, glancing at Charmaine's that she placed on top.

Mac's name was neatly printed in the emergency spot.

She realized Charmaine was still holding out her hand for the forms and not entirely sure what she was feeling, handed them over.

"I'm going to deliver everything to the accountant and the sheriff's office."

"You sure?" Charmaine asked. "I can probably drop the stuff by—"

"I got it." The phone on Charmaine's desk started ringing. "I have a few other things to take care of too, so I probably won't make it back this afternoon."

Charmaine nodded as she picked up the phone. "Thanks for calling Gold Creek—"

Delia left Charmaine's office. She packed up the material on her desk, pulled on her coat and headed out.

Across the street, the long trailer filled with tires was already gone.

Did it matter that Charmaine had listed Mac as her emergency contact?

The thought plagued her as she dropped off the security paperwork at the sheriff's department and continued plaguing her all the way to the other side of town where Emily Clay's accounting business was located at the end of a small strip of professional offices.

She parked next to an oversized pickup and went inside.

A handful of clients were waiting in the small lobby and Delia approached the receptionist. "I just need to drop these off. Employment forms from Gold Creek Recre—"

"Delia!" Emily stepped up beside the desk, smiling. Her dark hair was pulled back, showing off a narrow streak of silver. "Did we have an appointment today?"

Delia shook her head. "I was just dropping off the paperwork for the new employees at the rec center."

"Excellent." Emily took the thick folder. "I was thinking it was about time to start following up on that. Come on back to my office."

Delia glanced at the people who were waiting. "I don't want to interrupt your schedule."

"You're not," the older woman assured her. She headed down a carpeted hallway and Delia followed. "How are things going over there? Heard you stole Janie's best employee. All you ready for the big grand opening on Valentine's Day?"

"Now that we have a full staff roster, I think so.

And I don't know about stealing, but Charmaine has been a godsend." They passed three offices—all occupied with people sitting on both sides of the desks. When they reached the office at the end of the hall, Emily pushed the door wider and went in.

The office was twice the size of Delia's, which didn't say a whole lot, and was lined with file cabinets against one wall.

Emily dropped the folder on her desk and sat down behind it. "It always gets busier around here during tax season," she said. "But I have a couple of staff accountants now who handle most of it."

Delia perched on one of the chairs in front of the desk. "Is that Squire and Gloria?"

Emily turned in her chair, glancing at the collection of framed photographs displayed on her credenza. "It is, indeed." She plucked one toward the back and turned to face Delia again. "Good eye." Emily handed her the picture. "It's from the day they got married."

Delia studied the faces. They were both a lot younger. Both had fewer wrinkles but Squire's shock of gray hair had hardly changed and Gloria's auburn hair was only a little grayer now. "They look very happy."

"They were."

"And now?" She handed the photo back.

Emily didn't return it to her credenza but just held it in her hands. "I think they're trying to be happy but somehow, my father-in-law keeps getting in his own way." She smiled ruefully. "He's mellowed a lot but he's still the most stubborn person I know." She moved the frame back to its place on the credenza. "All I can do is wish you good luck working with him on that foundation with your grandmother."

Delia still didn't know what Squire and Vivian had discussed the evening before. "I'm not certain there still *is* a foundation," she admitted.

Emily cocked her head slightly. "Why?"

"Well, they can't agree on the time of day, for starters."

Emily smiled slightly. "Par for the course where Squire's concerned. He raised me, you know. From the time I was seven. You'd have thought he didn't have a speck of softness in him at the time, but when my parents died, he brought me home to that family of boys. A girl he was so distantly related to it wasn't really any relation at all. And he had *no* idea what to do with me. But he—all of them—became my home."

"I didn't realize there was a connection besides you being married to one of Squire's sons."

She smiled again. "Marrying Jefferson came later. And not without some drama of its own."

"Drama." Delia thought about Vivian again. "Did you know Squire's first wife?"

Emily shook her head. "Sarah died in childbirth with Tristan. None of us ever knew about the Templeton side of the family."

"I think my grandmother may have budged as much as she's capable of budging," Delia admitted. "She told me he's insisting on naming the foundation after Sarah. I don't think she'd even care about it except that she believes he's still rubbing her nose in the past."

"I love Squire dearly," Emily said on a sigh. "I'd like to say he's above that kind of motivation but who really knows?"

"Squire," Delia murmured. "He's the one who knows." She pushed to her feet. "Thanks for your time." Her gaze skated across the framed photographs. She recognized every single person in them.

Whether by blood or by marriage, they were all family.

She left Emily's office and returned to the mansion only to discover from Montrose that her grandmother had gone out with the Rolls.

"Where'd she go?"

"I'm not your grandmother's keeper," Montrose intoned.

"Back to normal, I see."

She went to the atrium and up to her old office, silently acknowledging how quickly it had become "old" since she'd started focusing her attention on Gold Creek.

She sat in the chair behind her desk and turned so she was looking out the window. The handprints she and Mac had left on the glass the week before had been polished away.

Undoubtedly the very next morning.

She rolled her chair close to the window and leaned her forehead against the thick, cool pane, thinking of him.

When her cell phone buzzed, she pulled it out of her back pocket. She smiled at the display and held it to her ear. "Did my thinking about you conjure up this call? You've made good time if you're already in Gillette."

"Can you get over to the garage?"

She sat up straight at the urgency in Mac's voice. "What's wrong?"

"I just got off the phone with Dave Ruiz. Someone tried setting fire to the place."

Horror froze her in place for a moment. But then she shoved out of the chair and ran out of the office. "What do you need me to do?" She raced down the stairs and nearly plowed into Montrose at the bottom.

She caught his arms. "Fire," she told him. "Mac's garage."

She didn't wait for his reaction. Just stepped around him and ran down the hall.

"How bad is it?" she said into the phone.

"Fire sprinklers did their job, and the fire department is still doing theirs. But I just want to make sure Loreen's okay. Dave says she's not hurt but she's refusing to leave. I'm about a half hour outta Gillette. Soon as I get to a spot I can turn around in, I'm heading straight back."

Delia had visions of the long, heavy trailer tipped on its side as a result of an urgent U-turn. "Just hold tight for a few minutes before you do anything. I'm on my way. I'll call you as soon as I'm there."

She heard relief in his sigh. "Thanks."

She pocketed her phone, retrieved her coat and left out the side door.

It didn't matter that Charmaine had listed Mac as her emergency contact.

Delia was pretty sure that Mac had just said that she was his.

Chapter Eighteen

She could see the flashing lights of the emergency vehicles blocking off Main Street long before she reached them.

She parked at the rec center and ran across the street, giving the firehoses snaking across the frozen ground a wide berth as she worked her way closer.

There was a lot of water arcing through the air. A lot of firefighters shouting instructions to each other.

She dragged her knit scarf up to cover her nose and block the acrid smell. She spotted Mac's office manager about the same time she spotted the flames still licking around the office portion of the building.

"Loreen!" She ran over to her. The woman looked shaken, with only a shiny foil blanket clutched around her shoulders. Delia pulled off her scarf and wrapped it around her. "Are you okay? You didn't get hurt?"

Loreen's teeth were chattering a little. Shock, Delia figured. "I'm o-okay."

"Let's find you a place to sit down."

"I don't want to leave—"

"Mac wouldn't want you standing here like this." She slid her arm around Loreen's waist. "Come on." The more distance they put between the smoke and that horrible smell, the better.

"All of our records," Loreen fretted. "It's all paper. Mac wanted me to use the computer but—"

"Don't worry about that. What he cares about is that you're safe. Watch the curb now." She tightened her hold as Loreen stumbled slightly. She was aiming for the convenience store because it was closer than her car or the rec center. "The only reason he sent me here was to make sure you were okay."

"He did?"

"We'll call him in a minute." She gestured at the two teenagers sitting on the cement bench outside the store. "Move over."

They'd been watching the excitement next door and they ungraciously shuffled aside, freeing up just enough space for Loreen.

The woman sniffled and wiped her eyes. "I know it's all my fault."

"Of course it isn't," Delia soothed. She hit the button on her phone to redial Mac and he answered immediately. "Loreen's okay," she said. "Do you want to talk to her?"

Even through the phone line and the noise of the fire engines nearby, she could hear the gruffness in his voice. "Yeah."

She handed Loreen the phone but kept her hand on the woman's shoulder for comfort.

"How long have you two been here watching?" The kids on the bench were still gawking at the spectacle. They weren't the only ones. At least two dozen people had gotten out of their vehicles, blocked by the closed-off street, to watch the scene unfolding.

"About half an hour. Stinks, don't it?"

In more ways than one, she thought, watching the smoke curling up into the cold, pale sky.

Loreen handed the phone back to Delia and she held it to her ear again. "I know you're worried, but the worst of it looks centered around the office." Of course, half of Mac's apartment was directly above the office, but she didn't want to bring that up.

He swore and it was one of the few times she'd ever heard him do so. "I still haven't found a place to turn my rig around."

She eyed the activity. Was it becoming slightly less frenzied? Or was that just her imagination being hopeful? "You're closer to Gillette than here. Keep going," she said. "Instead of dumping the trailer, you can leave it there. Surely, they won't mind under the circumstances. Plus, you'll make better time driving back without having to haul it anyway."

He swore again. "I know you're right but—"

"It's going to be okay, Mac. Nobody's hurt. Let's

keep it that way, okay? I love you, so just drive safely and let me know when you get to Gillette."

She hung up the phone only realizing what she'd said once it was too late.

Then she decided she didn't care.

She did love Mac Jeffries.

And if that didn't make her serious about him, she didn't know what did.

It took another hour before the hard, high arch of water spraying over the garage slowed. Dwindled. Stopped.

The nearly deafening noise of the fire engine dropped commensurately, too.

She watched the firefighters, fully geared up, traipsing around the building, boots splashing in the water that had pooled in the parking lot. It streamed into the street and flooded the gutters.

Considering the dropping temperature, they'd be lucky if it didn't freeze over before it had a chance to finally drain away.

The two kids had gone on their way and Delia and Loreen sat huddled together on the cold bench. It had gotten dark but the light from the store illuminated a wide circle around them. The clerk had offered them another blanket. It was stretched across their knees.

The blanket that Charmaine had produced from her trunk was around their backs. "I'd stay, too," she'd said, looking torn, "but the kids both have tests coming up."

"Go," Delia had told her. "There's nothing to be done here right now anyway."

"I'll check back in," she'd promised, and left.

Dave Ruiz, looking almost as tired as his mother, finally crossed over to them. His breath was a ring around his head. "Bringing in Toby Rutledge for questioning," he told them.

"Toby wouldn't do this," Loreen fretted. She'd told Delia about the young man coming into the office for his final paycheck shortly before she'd smelled smoke. "I don't care how angry he was about being fired, he wouldn't do this."

"We'll see." Dave's gaze flicked over the two of them. "Y'oughta go home, Ma. It's twenty-five degrees out here. Nobody's going into the garage any time soon. Not until the fire chief's done his investigation. Only thing you'll accomplish out here like this is to catch pneumonia."

"He's right." Delia squeezed Loreen's hands. "Mac's already on his way back."

"Toby wouldn't do this," Loreen said again, shaking her head dolefully. But she rose stiffly and let her son hand her into the back of another deputy's SUV. She couldn't take her own car because it remained blocked in the parking lot by the fire trucks that had yet to clear away.

Dave returned to Delia. "Fire department'll keep a crew here until they're certain there are no more hot spots. Was a good thing Mac had pulled out that trailer of old tires. Could have been a lot worse."

Delia looked past him to the damage. The firefighters had kept the fire from spreading beyond the first bay door closest to the office. But what hadn't been blackened by fire or burned down to bones was soaked in water.

"No reason for you to stay, either."

"I know." She stayed anyway, though she did return the blanket to the store. Then, with Charmaine's blanket wrapped around her coat like a big shawl, she crossed the street to sit and wait inside her car.

For the next hour, she cycled on and off her car engine, warming up the interior just enough to keep her going a little while longer while she kept Charmaine's blanket snugged up beneath her chin. It was good enough. And the seat was a lot better than cold concrete.

She'd set her phone on the dashboard where she could see it if Mac texted or called.

The *WEAVERFUNDS* notifications had reached nine hundred and eighty-three by the time the sheriff's department packed it up and left. With the roadblock lifted, traffic began to flow again.

She was surprised by the amount, given the time of night. A lot of vehicles drove up to the corner in front of her, idled a while and then turned back the way they'd come.

People were driving out to see the damage.

Then Mac's truck arrived.

He turned into his parking lot, and she saw the tailgate swing a little. The water that hadn't entirely drained away *was* icing over just as she'd expected.

He parked in front of the yellow tape crisscrossing

his building with as much abandon as the streamers at the rec center and got out. He planted his feet, arms akimbo. The headlights washed most of the color out of him. Even his hair looked lighter than it really was.

She jogged across the street once more.

Despite knowing the ice was forming, she still slipped precariously when she reached his parking lot. But at least she didn't land on her nose before she reached his side.

She was excruciatingly aware of what she'd told him on the phone, but more aware of how he must feel, looking at his business and his home in this condition. He'd mentioned how he'd taken over the garage when his uncle died but Loreen had told her how much work he'd put into it. Doubling the business. Tripling it. The number of times he'd gone without drawing a salary for himself because they needed another piece of equipment and he refused to owe the bank for any of it.

He slid his arm around her, pulling her closer. "Thanks." His voice was low.

She wrapped her arms around his waist and leaned her head against his shoulder. "For what?"

"Being here."

The tears glazing her vision felt hot. "I wouldn't be anywhere else."

Eventually they went back to Vivian's.

Montrose met them at the door, opening it wide. His only deference to the late hour was the black cardigan that had replaced the black suitcoat. "Can I get you anything, Mr. Jeffries?"

Mac shook his head. He walked through the foyer, his attention on the ground as if it was an effort to put one foot in front of the other.

"Thank you, Montrose," she murmured. "Would you mind rounding up a few things for Mac?" He'd had a change of clothes with him only because he'd intended on spending the night in Gillette, but that was it.

"I took the liberty of placing some items in your room earlier." The edges of Montrose's thin lips actually turned up in a smile.

Her eyes burned all over again. "Thank you," she whispered.

She caught up to Mac halfway up the staircase and they silently went to her room.

She'd left the bed in a mess that morning. It felt like a year ago. Now it was made up again. The duvet turned back invitingly. The pillows plumped and pristine.

She nudged him onto the side of the bed, vaguely alarmed that he went so easily.

"I can't believe Toby would do it. Thought I knew him."

She knelt at his feet and began tugging off his boots. "Maybe he didn't." She nearly fell back when the boot finally slipped free. She tossed it aside and reached for the other. "Nobody knows for sure what happened."

"They picked him up for questioning."

"Doesn't mean he's guilty." She tossed aside the second boot and straightened. "There were other people coming and going in your garage, too. Loreen told me Cadell did a half-dozen oil changes. Or maybe it wasn't even intentional at all."

"Ruiz said they've already identified the source of the fire."

Her chest squeezed. "Which was?"

"*That* he didn't tell me." His lips twisted. "Suppose they want to be sure I'm not the one torching my own damn garage."

"You know they don't think that."

"I don't know what to think," he said wearily and scrubbed his hands down his face, rasping over the stubble on his jaw that hadn't been there when he'd come by the rec center so many hours ago.

He ducked his head when she pulled his shirt up over his shoulders. She tossed it aside, but then picked it up again and spread it neatly over the upholstered bench at the foot of her bed.

When she turned back to him, he'd risen and was stepping out of his jeans.

Warmth slid through her veins, and she quickly looked away.

Now was *not* the time.

She took the jeans, shook them out and spread them next to the shirt. Then, as she was heading into the en suite, she heard a soft tap on the bedroom door.

She opened the door, expecting Montrose.

But Vivian stood on the other side.

She wore a pink quilted robe that buttoned from her neck to her toes and her silvery hair was newly cut in a stylish bob. Hairdresser, Delia thought. That's where Vivian had gone with the car earlier that day.

Or yesterday. Since it was well past midnight.

"I heard you were back," Vivian said.

Delia had lived in the house for four years. Not once had her grandmother ever visited her room. She wasn't sure that Vivian had ever even visited the entire west wing of the house, except, perhaps, when it had been completed. "We just got in a few minutes ago."

"May I?"

Delia sent a questioning look at Mac. He was sitting up against the pillows. Broad chest bare. Duvet hooked up over his waist. He didn't object, so Delia pulled the door wide.

Vivian entered. Her slippers had little puffs of feathers seemingly anchored by diamond-like pins. They peeped out from beneath her satiny robe with every step.

She stopped a yard away from the bench where Delia had laid out Mac's clothes. "I'm very sorry to hear about your auto repair shop. Montrose tells me the damage may not be *too* severe?"

"I'll know more tomorrow."

"Yes." She held her fingertips at her neck. "Once the insurance people have their say. Sometimes it feels as though they are in the ultimate control." She tapped her index finger lightly against her throat.

"It's a terrible feeling to see something you love destroyed like that. My father's violin shop once nearly burned to the ground."

Delia shot her a look. "You've never mentioned this before."

"One shouldn't dwell on unhappy memories."

Delia felt her eyebrows shoot up so high she probably grew an inch. "Are you kidding me? Dwelling on unhappy memories seems like the thing that gets you through the day!"

"Don't be ridiculous."

"I'm *not* being ridiculous." She propped her hands on her hips. "Making up for the past. Making up for your bad memories. What's the difference?"

"One of these days, you'll have regrets too, Delia. I simply want to ease the weight of mine before it's too late."

"Delia." Mac's voice was quiet. His gaze captured hers and she pressed her lips together, squelching her impetuous words. He held out his hand.

She took it and he gave it a warm squeeze.

"What happened with your father's shop?" he asked Vivian.

"An accident while preparing varnish." She shifted, clasping her hands at her waist. "No one was injured, but the damage to his business was something I've never forgotten."

"How old were you?"

"Seven." She gave a quick sigh. "I don't mean to keep you." She walked back toward the door. "If you need anything," her gaze flicked briefly to Delia, "please don't be shy."

"Thank you, Mrs. Templeton."

"I wish I could say it was my pleasure, dear, but considering the circumstances, it hardly seems pleasurable, does it?"

"No, ma'am."

Vivian put her hand on the doorknob. "Try and rest. You'll have much to do all too soon. Good night, Delia." Then she stepped out of the room and pulled the door closed with a soft click.

Delia looked at Mac. "I'll be back in a minute."

"Don't go after her and give her a hard time."

She leaned over the bed and gave him a soft kiss. "Vivian's champion now, are you?"

"Everyone needs one at one time or another." He kissed her fingertips and let her go.

She caught up to her grandmother before she'd made it to the end of the hallway. "Vivvie."

Her grandmother stopped as if startled. "Delia. What—"

"What went on between you and Squire yesterday?"

Her fingertips fluttered at the base of her neck again. "He told me he'd given up. I'd won. That I could name the foundation whatever I wanted. Use the money for whatever causes I chose." She pursed her lips. "Gracious of him, since it's mostly my money in the first—"

"He just gave up?" Delia snapped her fingers. "Like that?"

"I just said so, didn't I? Why are you bothering me with this when you have a healthy young man in your bedroom who surely needs some comfort, tonight of all nights?"

"Don't you wonder why Squire is giving up? After sixty years of a cold war, five years of outright battle, and six weeks—that I know of—engaged in this latest skirmish over the most basic decisions where the foundation is concerned, aren't you the least bit curious *why*?"

Delia waved her arms and continued. "You can't swing a cat in this town without knocking into one member or another of his family. *His* family. The same people that you have welcomed under this roof. The same people you've admired and supported. They hail from him. Can't you at least have enough respect for him to wonder why he has suddenly tossed in the towel?"

Her grandmother just stood there. Eyes narrowed. What she was thinking was anyone's guess.

Delia tossed up her hands and returned to her bedroom. She leaned back against the closed door, willing away her frustration with her grandmother and looked toward the bed.

Mac was asleep.

Her agitation drained away. She crept over to the bed and carefully drew the duvet up his chest. She kissed his brow where his hair was tumbled and held her breath when he sighed deeply and rolled to face the other side of the bed—her side—and dragged a pillow against his chest.

She straightened and pulled off her sweater as she headed into the bathroom only to do a double take at the sight of the items placed on the vanity alongside her toiletries.

Toothbrush still in a package.

Comb in the same state.

She picked up the stubby shaving brush sitting next to a shaving mug and razor and rubbed her thumb thoughtfully over the bristles as she picked up her sweater and deposited it in the hamper in her walk-in closet.

Several items of men's clothing hung from hangers on a portable clothing rack that she'd never seen before in her life.

She fingered the sleeve of one of the flannel shirts. Blue like his eyes. Then she studied the blue jeans hanging next to them. She could peg men's sizes the same way she could women's.

And she knew instinctively that everything would fit Mac perfectly.

"Montrose," she murmured.

She finished undressing, pulled on flannel pajamas that weren't even distant relations to the sexy stuff in her lingerie drawer, snapped off the light and climbed into bed beside Mac.

He sighed again and threw aside the pillow hugged against his chest to pull her into his arms instead.

It was, she was quickly learning, her favorite place to be.

Chapter Nineteen

In the cold light of day, the damage to Mac's garage didn't look as bad as he'd braced himself for.

Still, it wasn't *good*.

But as he and Delia worked their way through the building once the fire chief allowed them entry, he could tell that the firefighters really had done him a service.

The office and his apartment were decimated. But his tools and equipment and most of the inventory he kept in the garage was pretty much unharmed, if he didn't count the soot that covered nearly every surface. The vehicle lifts were intact. The tire changers and balancers looked okay. The diagnostics and the air compressors didn't seem affected.

The new tires on the racks would probably have

to go because they'd been nearest to the fire, but the steel racks holding them should be fine. So should the tow truck, though Mac might need to strip the seats out of the cab and replace them altogether because of the pervasive odor.

On a positive note, the fire hadn't reached his trucks parked in the back bays. A good thing, since he planned to sell them for a hefty profit at auction once he finished restoring them. They'd also seemed to escape the worst of the soot, though when Delia helped him push them out from the "protection" of the garage, they realized the vintage trucks bore the same stench as the tow truck.

Delia adjusted her blue mask, which matched the one he was wearing. "The smell is stuck inside my nose now."

"Think it's going to be a while before the smell gets back to normal."

Mac looked over the garage once more. It was waterlogged. Ceiling. Walls. Even the epoxy floor.

Mac knew it would all have to come down, come off, come up. Only then would they know if the structure beneath was salvageable.

The first one to show up at the garage after the fire chief was the claims adjuster from Mac's insurance company. He informed Mac that he'd left from Gillette before dawn. "Have two more incidents to investigate after this one," he said, before going over to the chief and huddling with him for a worrisome amount of time.

"I thought the fire department and sheriff did

the investigating," Delia murmured from behind her mask. "What happens if they come to different conclusions?"

"I just don't want to end up holding the bag whether they do or not."

"That won't happen."

"Been involved with a lot of fire damage claims, have you?" He regretted the words. "Sorry. I'm just—" He exhaled roughly.

She rubbed his arm. "I know, Mac. I know."

Eventually, the insurance guy finished talking with the fire chief and traipsed around taking pictures with his cell phone before approaching Mac once more for his statement.

Since he'd been on the highway halfway to Gillette, he didn't have a lot to contribute.

"Your office manager was here, though." The adjuster looked through his notes. "Loreen Ruiz."

"She reported the fire," Mac confirmed and provided Loreen's phone number when asked. "You can call her, but if I know her, she'll be by here soon enough." Not that he particularly wanted the adjuster hanging around if he was going to keep watching Mac as if he'd done something wrong.

"And you, miss?" The adjuster looked at Delia. "What's your role here?"

Delia's uncertain gaze flicked to Mac.

"Friend," he said. "Very good friend," he added, but he knew it was too little too late.

Something in her gaze had flickered and dimmed. Not that she moved away from his side or anything.

But the way she folded her arms over her chest spoke volumes.

"All right," the adjuster said, sliding his notepad into his coat pocket. "I think I have what I need from you. I'll just need statements from your manager and apprentice Caden—"

"Cadell."

"Cadell." The adjuster handed over a business card. "If you have any questions, leave a message or send an email. I'm usually able to respond within a week or so."

Comforting, Mac thought grimly. "How long's it likely to be before the claim's processed?" He gestured at the mess of his garage. "I've got a business to run here."

"It takes as long as it takes."

Even more comforting. "Don't think you'd feel the same way if I applied that theory to paying my insurance premiums."

"Look, you can get started on a few things now. Pull out the ruined wallboard, things like that. There are restoration companies that specialize in this sort of thing."

"Not in Weaver," Mac muttered, watching the insurance guy leave. He clawed his fingers through his hair.

"What do you think we should do now?" Delia had uncrossed her arms at least. She was chewing her lip as she took in the sad state of his garage.

"Same as we did with the trucks." He sighed. "Pull it all out."

They were doing exactly that when others started to arrive.

Not just curiosity seekers, though there were plenty of them.

But people who genuinely wanted to help.

His Tuesday crew, even though they were cutting school on a Friday to be there, and their parents, too. Loreen—swiping tears whenever someone spotted them—who confirmed she'd talked to the insurance guy by phone and that she'd merely repeated everything she'd already told the police. Cadell, who brought his dad with him. Then there was Charmaine and even Jed Dalloway, down off the mountain.

One by one, customers kept dropping by. Some pitching in to help. Some to offer meaningless words of encouragement and hang-in-there's. By the end of the day, everything that could be moved from the inside of the garage—from engine hoists and floor jacks to windshield wiper blades and gumballs for the penny gumball machine—had been relocated to his parking lot. From there, they packed stuff in boxes to be stored elsewhere while Loreen—with Delia coaching alongside her—started an inventory of everything on a tablet computer.

Inside the garage, Mac and Jed and several others had removed the ruined materials until the interior of the garage was reduced to a skeleton of studs.

He debated whether to leave the bay doors open to keep fresh air circulating inside; he didn't necessarily want to expose things he couldn't move to the elements and vulnerable to thieves. He had more than a hundred thousand invested in the equipment just sitting there. Admittedly, it would take a forklift at the very least to steal anything. But then, Toby hadn't tried stealing anything. He'd just tried burning it to the ground.

In the end, tired of the debate chasing around inside his aching head, Mac closed the doors and locked them.

The sheriff's department hadn't held Toby after they'd questioned him, but the kid knew he was under their watchful eye now. He'd be worse than a fool to revisit the scene of the crime.

At least the snowstorm that had been predicted hadn't shown up. It was one small blessing.

He looked at the boxes and equipment spread out over his parking lot. "I'll have to rent a storage unit."

"Not necessary." Delia straightened from where she'd been marking numbers on the side of the box. "I've already thought of the perfect spot for you."

Evidently, she'd forgiven him for the "friends… very good friends" comment.

"I think you might even be able to keep up some of your business," she added.

He raised his eyebrows. He wasn't the only mechanic in town, but his garage was the largest. He couldn't think of a single place that would be able to accommodate him. "Where?"

"My grandmother's garages."

"No." He shook his head immediately.

"She's already agreed. She's not using them for anything but the Rolls—"

"I said no."

"But—"

"Dammit, Delia, I'm not taking handouts from your grandmother!"

Her eyes narrowed. "I would have called it a *favor* but whatever."

"Call it whatever the hell you want. The answer is no."

"Mite shortsighted if you ask me."

They both whirled to see Squire Clay walking up behind them.

Mac grimaced. "Something I can do for you, Squire?"

The old man set his cowboy hat back an inch on his head and surveyed the garage. "Was going to get over here earlier but got held up." He gestured at the rows of packing boxes lined up in front of the bay doors. "What's all this?"

Mac told him.

"And Delia's got a temporary solution for where you can store it all?"

"I do." She sounded tart. "And not just store it, but maybe keep some of his business going. But of course he—" she threw out her arm in Mac's direction "—has decided to get stubborn all of a sudden."

"I stopped taking charity handouts when I was fifteen," he said flatly. "I'm not starting back up now. You might be the heiress, sweetheart, but I pay my own way."

She reared back. Her eyes narrowed to slits of hazel. "*Heiress?*"

"Hold up here now," Squire said.

"Stay out of this," Delia warned him.

He raised an eyebrow. "Quite the tone you're getting, Delia girl."

"Don't call her *girl*," Mac warned.

Looking annoyed with the both of them, Squire settled his hat and strode back to the truck he'd left parked near the curb.

"Now look what you've done," Mac muttered. "Made me offend my biggest customer when it's the last thing I should be doing."

"I didn't make you do anything," she snapped, and she too turned on her heel and strode away, barely waiting to make sure the road was clear before running across the street and marching down the driveway to the rec center.

He picked up the nearest object—a crescent wrench as long as his arm—and heaved it at his garage.

The wrench shattered the last piece of office window that hadn't already been broken by the fire.

"See you're still prone to tantrums," a voice called out.

"God save me from people coming up behind me, unannounced," he muttered, recognizing the voice all too easily.

He looked back to see his brother, Dev, sitting in a pickup truck as old as the ones Mac restored.

His brother was parked at the side of the road with no regard for the fact that he was facing the wrong way. He had his arm propped on the opened window.

"What're you doing here?"

Dev got out. "Heard about your little fire." He wasn't as tall as Mac, but he'd always been stronger. "Thought I'd drive over and see the damage."

It wasn't like Cradle Creek was a hop-skip down the road. It was a five-hundred-mile jaunt. "How'd you hear?"

"You know. Rasmussen grapevine." Dev had a stained ball cap on his head and a wooden toothpick clenched between his teeth. He stopped next to Mac and studied the garage. "Helluva mess." He took out the toothpick and pointed it at the regurgitated contents from inside the garage. "Looks like Shippers-R-Us dumped a load on your front doorstep."

"And I need to get it off my front doorstep." He looked across the street. Delia had disappeared inside the rec center.

He turned and kicked a box.

"That helping?"

"No." He dug his fingers into the back of his neck. He didn't lose his temper often. "I feel like I'm watching twenty years of my life slip down the crapper."

"Know who did it?" The toothpick was back between Dev's teeth. He was squinting at the garage.

Mac told him about Toby and having to fire him. "I still can't believe he'd do it but he's the only one's got cause for a grudge."

"Y'always were unforgiving about your rules."

Mac sighed. He looked over at the rec center again. The banner had gone up that day advertising the grand opening, and he hadn't even noticed it. "Where're you staying, Dev?" He smiled humorlessly. "My guest couch is outta commission these days."

"Cozy-Night'll do me."

It was going to have to do Mac, too, if he didn't want to sleep in his truck.

Wasn't like Delia would be welcoming him into her west wing any time soon.

He scrubbed his hands down his face. "Ever think about getting married, Dev?"

His brother looked genuinely horrified. "What for? You get some girl knocked up?"

He wished he hadn't asked. Wished he didn't already have thoughts gnawing at him about Delia's family making a baby pool for a baby *they'd* created.

"You're here. So help me pull this stuff back in the garage." After all the work of removing everything just so he could peel his walls and roof back to the studs, it seemed the height of irony to be putting it all back again.

"I can still see his truck over there," Charmaine said, standing in the lobby of the rec center.

Even though it was after midnight, she was still there with Delia. Her kids were spending the night with their friends, she'd said. The only thing waiting for her at home was an empty house.

"He can sleep in his cold truck for all I care," Delia muttered. She was sitting on the floor filling heart-shaped plastic containers with gummy bears and jelly beans and dropping them into little white treat bags to be handed out at the grand opening.

Charmaine sat on the floor nearby and wrapped her arms around her upraised knees. "Did you hear any more news from the sheriff's department?"

"Nope." Delia reached for another plastic heart and felt only air. She looked in the box. Empty.

"Have any more containers?"

"Yes, but we've already filled five hundred treat bags with plastic hearts, coupons for free ice cream at Udder Huddle, pet grooming at Poocheez and cinnamon rolls at Ruby's Dinner. Plus dental floss and hand sanitizers. I'm sure that's going to be more than enough for the grand opening." She reached over to grab the little scoop Delia had been using for the candies and dumped some into her hand. "In fact, I'm worried that we'll have way too many. I'm already having nightmares about being strangled by streamers and choked by heart-shaped candies."

"It's a party," Delia said. "I keep telling you. People always come out for parties in Weaver." She pinched the bridge of her nose. "His truck is really still there?"

"Where'd you expect him to go?"

"I don't know!" She shot Charmaine a look. "Maybe to your house. You guys are such close friends—"

"I told you Mac and I weren't that sort of close."

"I'm not doing this again." Delia viciously decapitated a gummy bear with her front teeth.

"Doing what?"

"Chase after a guy who isn't interested in getting caught!"

"Pardon me, but I thought you'd *caught*—" Charmaine air-quoted the word "—each other plenty of times now."

"That's just sex." Delia held up one of the hearts. "I want this."

"Jelly beans and gummy bears."

"Love!"

Charmaine was smiling slightly. "Don't think love comes in a plastic heart, hon. Leastwise it never has for me."

"You don't understand. He called me an *heiress*. What he really meant was *spoiled*."

"That's it?" Charmaine waited a beat. "Big deal. Better than a lot of other terms I could name, having been personally called them all by my sleaze of an ex-husband."

Delia pushed restlessly off the floor and paced over to the doors. She cupped her hands against the glass and looked out. Sure enough, thanks to the light cast by the all-night convenience store, she could see the outline of Mac's truck parked in front of his garage.

"All I wanted to do was help," she said. "My grandmother's garages seemed so perfect. They're almost as big as Mac's place and just sitting there doing nothing. I don't know why it was so offensive to him. I never even got to tell him about my idea for his Tuesday troop." She looked at Charmaine. "What if we outfitted the storage shed out back with some automotive equipment? Instead of sacrificing garage time for paying customers in order to work with the kids, Mac could meet them here."

Charmaine nodded thoughtfully. "I'm a little offended I didn't think of that before you."

"Yeah, well, maybe if *you* proposed the idea, he wouldn't dismiss it out of hand."

"It wouldn't have to be just temporary, either," Charmaine added. "Once the garage is rebuilt, I mean. It could be a regular thing. Mac's always having to turn down kids the sheriff tells him about."

"Exactly. And if the program were *here*, Mac wouldn't have all the red tape on his plate. It'd be on Gold Creek's plate."

"Maybe you should tell him that."

She pushed off the floor. "Maybe I should."

"Well, don't forget this." Charmaine held out Delia's cell phone.

She started to push it into her pocket. But the display was lit up.

midnight-to-noon alert. ali at hospital. take two.

Mac heard the throaty car engine and lifted his head off the jacket he'd jammed under his head as a pillow.

The headlights of the Porsche swept over his truck as it turned onto Main. Delia was heading toward town, not her grandmother's mansion.

It was nearly one in the morning.

Where was she going at one in the morning?

He turned the keys in the ignition and followed.

The streets of Weaver at that hour were nearly empty. She flew through the green light, and it belatedly dawned on him that she was heading to the hospital.

Was one of her cousins having a baby?

Maybe it wasn't a false alarm this time.

He almost turned around to go back to guarding what was left of his garage.

He didn't.

He parked across the street from the hospital and watched until Delia had parked her own car near the emergency room entrance. He watched her hurry inside the building.

When she hadn't emerged a half hour later, he pulled out onto the street again and drove back to the garage.

Across the street, the rec center was dark. Even Charmaine had gone home.

He bunched his jacket beneath his head again and closed his eyes.

But he still didn't sleep.

His arms felt too empty.

Chapter Twenty

"Welcome to Gold Creek Recreation Center!" Delia smiled brightly as she handed out three more treat bags to guests. "And Happy Valentine's Day." She gestured to the reception desk. A balloon arch was suspended above it. "Enter the drawing for a year's free membership right over there."

She smiled at Maia who was doing the exact same thing as Delia, only on the other side of the doorway.

Music was playing from the loudspeakers. There were people milling around everywhere inside and outside the rec center. The weather was sparkling clear and not too bitingly cold. A long line snaked around the bounce house where it was positioned on a quarter of the parking lot.

The rest of the parking lot was filled with vehicles of every size and model.

Charmaine was giving tours, and Vivian was holding court—literally—on the basketball court as she and Nick Ventura described the inspiration behind the rec center's opening to Gerty Tomlinson for the next issue of *The Weaver Gazette.*

"I cannot *believe* it happened again," she heard Ali complaining as she and Grant came in with Reid. The little boy's cheeks were flushed from his time in the bounce house. "Two false alarms now! I won't be able to show my face at the hospital when I really *do* go into labor."

"Deeya!" Reid aimed for her and nearly took her down when he slammed against her legs, wrapping his strong little arms around her knees. "I bounced so high!"

"I bet you did, buddy." She was still teetering a little, holding her big tray of treat bags aloft. She was very certain that he needed no extra stimulation, but she handed him a treat bag anyway. "Give that to Mommy."

He was such a sweetheart, he trotted right back to Ali, offering the gift.

"Give Mommy an extra for her misery," Ali said, holding out her hand.

Delia gave her another bag. "Next time, don't go to the hospital until your water breaks."

Ali rolled her eyes and grabbed Grant's hand. Reid had spotted the balloons and was making a beeline for them.

Delia turned back to the door. There'd been a never-ending stream of people coming through since the judge cut the ceremonial ribbon they'd stretched across the front of the building. Now, Maia and Delia were down to their last batch of treat bags.

If she didn't count her misery every time she let her gaze stray to the garage across the street, the afternoon was an unqualified success.

"Look out," Maia warned without dropping her bright smile. "Collision coming at two o'clock."

Delia didn't realize what she meant until she saw Gloria Clay approaching the door from one direction and Squire Clay from the other.

Gloria was with her granddaughter April Dalloway and Squire was with Casey and Jane.

And they all hit the entrance at the same time.

Delia hadn't seen Squire since that night at Mac's.

Not that he was giving anyone, including her, any attention. That was reserved entirely for his wife.

Delia and Maia doled out treat bags as they all entered. She was just glad to see the tentative smile that Gloria sent Squire's way.

"What a coincidence seeing you here." Gloria plucked the plastic heart out of her bag and shook it lightly.

Squire's smile was thin. Wary. "You going to throw your heart at me, too?"

Gloria's smile wilted. "I threw my heart at you more than thirty years ago, remember?"

"I caught it, too," Squire muttered, "though you seem to forget that."

She tucked her hand through April's arm. "I want to see the pool." Her voice was husky. "I used to swim often back when your mother was a child."

Squire shot his grandson a look. "Suppose *this* was why you were so all-fired set on coming to this shindig right this minute? You knew your grandma was coming, too? Did you cook this up with April?"

"I cooked it up," Vivian said coolly, stopping next to Delia, surprising her. She hadn't realized her grandmother had left the basketball court. "I asked April and Casey to ensure you both landed in the same place at the same time," Vivian added.

Squire looked stymied, Gloria confused.

Delia leaned toward her grandmother. "What are you doing?"

"You've wanted us to choose a name for the foundation," Vivian said. "And I have."

Squire's expression tightened.

"It will be named exactly as you wish, Squire. The Sarah Benedict Foundation for Women and Children."

Gloria's lips twisted. "Very fitting." She tugged at April's arm. "The pool—"

"I thought you'd be pleased." Squire's voice was rough. "That's what you wanted, wasn't it? For me to end the war with *her*?" He waved his walking stick in Vivian's direction, not seeming to mind in the least that they were drawing everyone's attention. "What more proof do you need than me *partnering* with her?"

Gloria tossed her head back and stomped right

back to him. "The only thing you've proven—" she jabbed him with a finger "—is that even after all these years, your beloved Sarah still comes first!" She jabbed him a second time. "I've *always* known that she was the love of your life. I've lived with it." *Jab.* "Accepted it." *Jab.* "You still want to humiliate Vivian the way she once humiliated Sarah. Knock yourself out." *Jab.* "But I want no part of it and if you think for one *second* that I am *pleased*—" Her voice went hoarse and she went to jab him again, but he caught her finger.

"Dammit, woman, I am not a *pincushion*!"

It was like watching a train wreck, Delia thought dimly. Nobody seemed able to look away. Not even her.

"Sarah was a good wife. I loved her from the moment I met her." Squire's voice was tight. Hard. "When she died, I would've bargained with the devil if I could have brought her back. *You* chose to leave me. You said I couldn't change. Well, I can. There's only *one* love of my life! I'm looking at her and if she still can't see that the only reason I'm in league with Vivian—" he practically spit the word "—is because of her, then she's not as smart as I always believed."

Gloria's mouth parted. She was clearly shocked. "You've never said that before." She seemed to realize how they'd become the center of everyone's attention and smoothed her hair back with a hand that trembled.

"Said what?" Squire sounded more cantankerous than ever. "That you're smart? That you're my *wife*, even though you seemed to have forgotten it?"

"Shut up, you old fool," she muttered and went into his arms. "You're the love of my life, too," she said thickly and yanked his head down to kiss him.

Casey hooted. April laughed and clapped her hands.

And so did everyone else.

Delia looked away, dashing a tear from her cheek. She caught her grandmother's attention. "You planned this?" she asked under her breath.

Vivian looked resigned. "If anyone is going to make a scene, I prefer it to be me. You should know that by now, dear."

But when she turned away, she had a small smile on her face.

Dear Arthur, Delia thought. He'd be pleased.

She blinked hard and turned back to the crowd that had formed. She held up a fistful of treat bags. "Everybody out of the doorway, please," she said brightly. "We've got people trying to get in."

"Yeah," Casey drawled, doing his best to urge everyone to move along. "Gonna give Gold Creek a reputation as the geriatric love connection, here."

Mac saw the Rolls-Royce turn into his parking lot and muttered an oath. Even without seeing Vivian behind the wheel, he'd have known it was her just because of the way she bumped over the curb before coming to a stop.

He finished dumping his shovelful of heavy, wet

ash into the barrel as he watched her step gingerly around a pile of sodden, sooty rags. "Take a break, Cadell."

His apprentice put down his shovel and left them alone.

"Good afternoon, Mac." Vivian hailed him with a little wave. "Would you have a moment of time for me?"

He folded his arms over the top of his shovel handle. "Just out of curiosity, Mrs. Templeton, what would you say if I told you no?"

She looked surprised for a moment, then laughed. "I do see why Delia's so taken with you."

Mac grimaced. He'd slept two nights in his truck before deciding he was being too paranoid about Toby. Then he'd checked into the room at the Cozy-Night that Dev had just checked out of since his brother needed to get back home to Cradle Creek. Mac had been there since.

Four nights.

Alone.

Thinking about Delia.

"She doesn't seem real taken with me lately."

Vivian waved a dismissive hand. Her bright eyes were focused on what remained of his garage. "She's a lot like me. But—" she gave him a quick, direct look "—lest that scare you off, she learns more quickly than I ever did."

"Mrs. Templeton—"

"Vivian." She took a step closer to the barrel and looked inside, her nose wrinkling, then stepped back.

"You really should consider using my garages. What good are they doing sitting empty?"

"No disrespect, ma'am, but you've got an entire house sitting mostly empty."

She smiled and toyed with her fur collar. "I understand your insurance isn't being terribly cooperative. Using the ongoing arson investigation to delay settling your claim."

"What *I* don't understand is why you know about *my* insurance."

"The privilege of being old and nosy." She gave him a sudden, very direct look that made ice dribble down his spine. "I have a proposition for you."

He waited warily.

"I will speak to a few people. See what can be done to move along your claim. If I'm successful, you'll agree to move your tools and whatnot into my garages which—" she raised her hand when he opened his mouth "—I will rent to you for a reasonable sum, along with the guesthouse next to it. You will have a place to live, and a place to work until you're able to rebuild here."

"If you're *not* successful?"

"Then you can continue trudging along your merry way, shoveling ash and sleeping in that dreary motel."

"What, exactly, is a reasonable sum where you're concerned?"

"I wasn't always wealthy, you know. Not like this. We had some standing. My father was well-respected. But not rich. That didn't come until I married my first husband."

"Does Delia know you're here?"

"Good Lord, Mac. I thought you were smart. Of course not. I know you own this property outright, but what did your average utilities cost?"

He rubbed the back of his neck. She was giving him a headache. But he was curious enough to see where the bread crumbs led to tell her.

"Double that and we'll call it a reasonable sum," she said crisply. "Can you afford that?"

He dropped his hand. "Seeing as how you're apparently right in my business, you know I can. As long as I have the ability to keep work coming in." He could also keep paying Cadell and Loreen.

"Lovely." She poked around in the handbag she was carrying in the crook of her arm and extracted a cell phone. "If you'll pardon me for just a moment." She dialed and held the phone to her ear. "Stewart? Have you taken care of that little matter we discussed this morning? Regarding Mr. Jeffries." She waited a moment, then gave a satisfied nod. "Well done, dear. And you'll be back in time for my little soiree? Until then." She returned the phone to her purse and focused on Mac once more. "I'll leave you to start your packing and such. Meanwhile, I have another visit to make."

Could she magically light a fire under the insurance company's collective ass with a simple phone call? He didn't like her in his business at all, but if she succeeded, he wasn't inclined to debate the point.

He watched her pick her way back toward the Rolls-Royce. "Amy Rutledge," Vivian said over her shoulder. "Delia suggested I talk to her about coming to work for me."

Mac didn't think he could be more surprised, but he was. "When did she tell you that?"

"At the grand opening. She seemed to be quite certain you would approve of the idea despite this horrible business with the fire and her son's alleged involvement. That you would still want to encourage Amy's independence." She pulled open the car door. "Was Delia wrong?"

It wasn't often Mac felt bemused. But he did now. "No. She wasn't wrong."

"Do I turn at the third street up or the fourth to get to the Rutledge home?"

He cleared his throat. "Fourth."

Cadell returned after she'd departed, bumping the Rolls yet again over the curb in a way that made Mac wince. "She's something else, isn't she?"

Mac's phone vibrated and he pulled it out of his back pocket.

It was the insurance company.

"Something else," he murmured, looking at the taillights heading down the road.

And Delia was too.

Chapter Twenty-One

"All right." Delia spread the full-color poster-boards across the dining room table in front of her grandmother and Squire. "Each one of these boards represents a page of the new Sarah Benedict Foundation website. The home page, describing the basic mission—supporting our neighbors and improving lives. Then the three categories we're going to be funding. Women and Children. Education. Entrepreneurship." She tapped each one in turn. "Everything is clean. Simple. To the point. Each category selected leads to further explanation as well as the grant application forms. Every form will be available in multiple languages for greater accessibility. And we'll be doing rolling funding so that means applicants can submit at any time throughout the year. I anticipate announcing the first of the grant recipients in each category by the beginning of June."

Vivian settled her reading glasses on her nose. "We agreed we were strictly funding issues relating to women and children."

"And I'm overriding you," Delia said smoothly.

Her grandmother sat back in her chair, her eyebrows rising slightly. "Are you now?"

"I am." She glanced at Squire, sitting in the chair next to Vivian. His cowboy hat was on the table between them, but he didn't look as if he were in any hurry to grab it and go, which is how most of their previous meetings had gone.

Now that his wife had moved back in with him, his mood had improved noticeably.

She picked up her phone and showed the display. "Twenty-two hundred and thirteen inquiries at *WEAVERFUNDS*," she said. "I paid attention to every single one." Including Mac's, which had been the twenty-two hundred and fourteenth submission. Coming in just the night before.

Which she couldn't think about if she wanted to get through her presentation without falling apart.

She cleared her throat. "After excluding the requests that were purely nonsense, there were roughly seventeen hundred legitimate requests for assistance."

She set her phone aside and picked up another posterboard with the graph she'd put together. "That's seventeen hundred in a mere thirty-six days! Sixty-two percent from nonprofits in Wyoming. Another six percent in neighboring states and twelve in other states." She frowned slightly when a loud noise reverberated through the dining room. "The remaining twenty percent came from individuals. Broadly speaking, they addressed needs within one of these three categories. Given the numbers right here in our own region, there's a clear need that I believe we can help meet."

She slid the board in front of them atop the others. "So those are the categories we're going with. I've confirmed with our website designer that we're ready to launch—what *is* that noise?" She looked at Vivian. "Please tell me you haven't launched another one of your construction projects. Montrose threatened to quit three times when you built those additional bedrooms last year."

"I'm doing nothing of the sort," Vivian assured her. "What types of educational funding are you suggesting?"

"Collaborating with existing programs to increase early learning, adding extracurricular activities that promote health and safety, adult learning, scholarship opportunities for trade schools as well as univers—" She broke off at yet another loud sound from outside and went to look out the window. She saw nothing unusual, though. Just the sweep of smooth snow at the rear of the house.

She returned to the table. "Anyway, as I was saying, we're ready to launch on the first of the month. That's a week and a half from now. I've been working with a PR firm that Gage recommended on our promo. We've arranged interviews with you both for—"

"Interviews. Hell no." Squire shook his head. "Your granny can do all that. She's the one who likes to talk people's ears off."

"I'll overlook the *granny* comment." Vivian was holding up one of the boards to get a closer look at the montage-style images. "This looks very impressive, Delia."

"Thanks. The promotional rounds will begin on the last day of the month. Local news channels. Several radio stations. We want to get the word out, obviously, about what we're doing. Also, all those who've submitted info through *WEAVERFUNDS*—even the ridiculous ones—are being sent direct links to the appropriate info page at the new website so they can submit proper grant proposals. Everyone will receive the same treatment and objective review."

"Not everything can be objective, dear."

"We're going to try our best, Vivvie. I'll wait to shut down the site altogether until the new one goes live." Another crash made the floor seem to vibrate.

"That's it." She pushed through the door into the kitchen.

Montrose was sitting at the counter, headphones on, glued to another episode of *Downton Abbey* on his tablet. He didn't even give her a glance.

She strode through the house, snatching an ancient sweater off a hook by the side door, and went outside.

A moving truck with a ramp sticking out the back

was parked in the courtyard. She walked around it suspiciously. Delia knew Stewart was coming back to town because she'd given him the rundown on the final details of the website. Was he moving into the guesthouse permanently?

She heard another one of those gunshot-loud claps and nearly jumped out of her skin.

The two skinny guys carrying boxes down the ramp of the moving truck, on the other hand, didn't even seem to notice. "Hey." She skipped toward them to get their attention. "Who's in charge?"

One of them jerked his thumb over his shoulder.

Mac stood in the shadow cast by Vivian's six-car garage. Three of the six doors were open, displaying the yawning space inside. But it wasn't empty; it contained a vehicle lift that looked sized to lift a bus if it needed to.

Her heart jittered around inside her chest.

Since Valentine's Day, the temperature had jumped up to wildly comfortable forty-degree days. He wore only a long-sleeved shirt with his jeans. A blue shirt that fit his wide shoulders perfectly. A blue shirt that matched his eyes.

She pulled the threadbare sweater more tightly around her shoulders as she slowly crossed toward him.

Even though she'd delivered the things Montrose had arranged over to the office at the Cozy-Night when Charmaine had told her he'd checked in there, she hadn't seen him in nearly a week.

Not since he'd accused her of being an heiress.

"What's going on?"

He lifted his arms. "What's it look like?"

She pressed her lips together and jumped again at another loud bang.

The big metal legs of the lift were being fastened into the concrete, she realized. Two guys were crawling around the base of the four legs with huge compressor guns in their hands.

She cleared her throat. "It looks like you've seen the value of my offer."

"Vivian's offer," he corrected. "She came to see me."

Delia closed her eyes for a moment. "I told her to stay out of it." When she opened her eyes again, his blue gaze was roving over her face.

"Think that's like telling the sun not to rise in the morning. We came to an equitable agreement." He was silent for a moment. The two moving guys circled around them, clomping up the ramp of the truck. They emerged again and clomped down the ramp toward the garage.

"I've missed you," he said quietly.

She lifted her chin. "Surprising when I'm so spoiled."

"I never called you spoiled."

"May as well have."

He exhaled softly. "You told me you loved me."

Her eyes stung. "And you didn't say anything."

He touched her hair. Slid it behind one ear. "I was staring at the ashes of my life's work. What did I have to offer you, Delia?"

She dug her fingers into her arms, trying not to tremble and failing miserably.

She looked down at the cobblestones beneath their feet. "You didn't have to offer me anything. But you didn't have to just dismiss my idea about setting up your business here."

"I've worked hard for every single thing I've ever gotten." His voice was husky. "I don't know how to be any other way than I am. That's how I used to sleep at night."

"I don't want you to be any other way." She blinked but the tears still escaped the corners of her eyes.

"And I don't want you to be any other way, either. But you need to understand why I can't just take handouts—*favors*—that easily."

"You made a submission at *WEAVERFUNDS*." She had to push the words past the knot in her throat.

"I told you I'd think about it."

"You don't think that'd be a favor? Getting funding from the foundation so you could take the time to work with more kids?"

He looked frustrated. "I don't know. The funding wouldn't be for *me*. It'd be for the kids." He thrust his fingers through his hair. "Your idea about your grandmother's garage *was* good. Sweetheart, all your ideas are good. But when it comes to my business, I need to know I'm holding up my side of things, too. I'm paying Vivian rent. Just until the garage gets rebuilt. Then things'll go back to normal."

She decided her good idea about the rec center

and his Tuesday troop could save for a little while. "And us? What's normal for us?"

His eyes searched hers. "What do you want normal to be, Delia?"

"Anything as long as it's with you," she whispered.

The corners of his lips curved up. He took her hands in his and reeled her closer. "Then we'll be the two most normal people on the face of the planet." He smiled slightly. "Not exactly a sweeping declaration there, but—" He cleared his throat. "I love you, Delia Templeton. And I used to sleep just fine at night, knowing who I was. Who I am. Until I met you. And now, the only way I'm sleeping well is if you're beside me."

He turned until she was facing the guesthouse. "That's where I'm going to live. For now. Question is, will you live there with me? Sleep with me? Smile with me? Laugh?" He thumbed the tears slipping from her eyes. "Cry with me?"

"Yes."

"And after that? When all this mess with the garage is straightened out? I don't expect you to live over it in a one-bedroom apartment. We'll find a house. Big enough for us. And maybe more. Or a piece of land. We can build—"

"Anything," she said thickly and knew what it felt like to have a man look at her with his heart in his eyes. And know down in her soul that the same love was shining from her own. "Anything," she repeated. "Anything as long as it's with you."

His arms surrounded her and his mouth grazed hers. "Always?"

"Always." She wrapped her arms around his shoulders. "As long as an infinity."

Epilogue

The full Templeton family contingent showed up at Vivian's soiree the next evening.

"Have you ever seen two more uncomfortable-looking souls?" Season clucked her tongue softly.

Delia looked across Vivian's living room where everyone had gathered for cocktails. Hayley was leaning over a chair as if she couldn't quite bear the weight of holding herself upright while Stewart had Seth cornered in conversation nearby. Ali was on a couch with her feet up, fanning herself with a napkin. Grant was beside her, absently rubbing her feet while he listened to Mac talk about Delia's idea of his Tuesday troop operating out of the rec center.

She'd finally gotten around to sharing it with him in the wee hours that morning.

As if Mac felt her attention, he looked her way and smiled. Warmth spread through her.

Maybe this time next year, they'd be the ones waiting for a baby to arrive.

"I don't know about uncomfortable," Archer said. "I just know I lost fifty bucks yesterday 'cause neither one of them cooperated by having a baby."

"Have a little compassion." Nell pulled his arm around her. "You remember what those last few weeks were like."

"Hot peppers," Rory said. "That's what I had to resort to." She had another wrap around her torso holding baby Thea. This time the scarf was a swirl of watery blues and greens.

Meredith had obviously overheard them. "The babies will come the day after tomorrow. Midnight-to-noon. I told you. I had a dream all about it." She nibbled one of the canapés sitting on the napkin that Carter held. "Where is Vivian, anyway?" She looked to Delia. "I thought she'd be down by now."

"You know our Vivvie. She's the only one who likes to make an entrance even more than I do."

"We're leaving in forty-five minutes, regardless," Carter said.

"Why don't you check on her, Delia," her mom suggested. "Even for Vivian this is a bit much."

"We won't use the time to grill the boyfriend," Archer said, "but I can't make any promises about your dad or your brother."

Both of whom had been polite enough when she'd walked into the party with Mac by her side, but had that sort of set look in their expressions that she knew only too well. She wasn't worried. Mac could handle them.

"You'd better be quick," her mom advised humorously.

Delia stopped near Mac as she went. "I'm going to try to hurry my grand—"

Vivian swept into the room. She wore a silver dress and had a champagne glass in one hand and a wicker basket in the other. "Good evening, my darlings! I'm so glad you've all come. Delia, dear." She held out the basket. "Pass these out. One to your brother and each of your cousins. The one left over will be for your sister."

Delia took the basket and lifted one of the red hearts out of it. Leftovers from those they hadn't used at the grand opening. Complete with candies inside. They rattled when she shook it. "What're you up to?"

"Solving a long-standing problem." Vivian didn't wait to see that Delia complied but walked further into the room. "You can choose your own heart," she said. "Or have Delia choose for you. She doesn't know anything more about the contents than you do. When you have yours, I'll ask you to refrain from opening it for now."

"What new game have you come up with, Mother?" Delia's father sounded weary.

"You needn't worry about it, David. Nor you, Carter. Your positions are crystal clear."

Nothing was clear, but when Vivian talked like that, it was wise to be wary. Delia carried the basket over to Ali first, who reached blindly into the basket. Delia moved around the couch.

She leaned down toward Mac when she walked around him. "Warned you." She dropped a heart in his hand. "Mac's holding my heart," she announced to the room at large.

"Pretty sure that's not all he's held," Ali said.

Delia laughed. After all, it was true. She finished passing out the hearts, then gave Vivian the basket and went to sit next to Mac.

He wrapped his arm around her. "Look." He turned his phone so she could see the text message. It was from Dave Ruiz.

toby rutledge innocent.

arson charges filed tonight against eddie macdonald.

caught on video. already confessed.

She exhaled. "I'm so glad for you."

"Be glad for Toby," he said under his breath.

"I know you're going to give him another chance and hire him back," she whispered.

"We'll see." But there was a faint smile around his lips that she knew very well now.

Vivian was walking through the living room, turning the last heart between her fingers. "It's become increasingly apparent that nobody wants the responsibility of my money when I'm gone," she began bluntly. "I have rafts of accountants and attorneys—so-called experts—continually advising me on what will best protect my interests all while they get to line their pockets. No slight intended to you or your father, Stewart."

Delia glanced toward him. He was the only one in the room who didn't look wary.

She didn't know whether that was a good sign or not.

"While the matter of making sure my first husband's inheritance benefits his sister's descendants the way he'd intended was rectified a few years ago, there still remains the matter of *my* estate and how it can be best used."

"Aren't you doing that with *WEAVERFUNDS*?"

"If you don't mind, Archer, that's the Benedict Foundation," Delia corrected tartly.

"Look who's gotten all grown up and feisty." He grinned.

Vivian rattled her heart loudly. "Unruly children. This is important. The foundation with Squire is a separate matter. But the theory is very much the same."

"Get to the point, Mother." The only time Delia ever heard her dad sound impatient was when he was dealing with Vivian.

"The remainder of my personal estate—including the mansion—has been rolled into what is now the Archer-Finley Trust. This trust will continue to endow the Finley Library and Gold Creek, as well as the Weaver Hospital. And hopefully many more admirable efforts in the future. I don't believe there is anyone here who would argue the merits of that." She held up the heart again. "Inside each of these is a flash drive containing a much more complete explanation of what I'm telling you now. Plus, a piece of paper that says either yes or no. Four hearts with yes. Five with no. Yes means you will serve as trustee for the Trust. No means you're relieved of that duty."

She waited while the murmurs rippled around the room. "As you can see, this is entirely random. No favoritism. However, if you receive a no and would *like* to volunteer, you will be gladly accepted. On the other hand, if you receive a yes but refuse to act as a trustee, you will not be allowed to change your mind. Once you give up the right, there is no turning back. In other words, there could be as many as nine of you serving as trustees. Or as few as none." She drew in a breath. "Any questions on this point?"

"What happens if a trustee dies?"

"All of that is explained in the document on the flash drive," Vivian said. "Suffice it to say if you're a trustee and wish to leave your position to your own beneficiary, you may do so." She looked around the room. "Anything else? All right then. There's just one last thing. Because there is always one last thing, of course. Whether any of you serve or do not serve, none of you will personally receive any financial benefit from the Archer-Finley Trust."

She walked over to Carter and David where they were standing near the fireplace. She looked up at them both. "Not you, David." Her voice was quiet.

"Not you, Carter. Not your children. Not your children's children. I know you'll never believe I only ever wanted the best for you. My methods were wrong when you were young. No doubt you'll read me chapter and verse about how wrong they are now. You grew up believing our wealth was the source of all our ills. So, I'm removing the possibility of that truth for once and for all. And that's it. I love you all. And to prove it—" she tossed her head back and drained her champagne glass "—I've cut every single one of you out of the will."

Then she looked around. "Montrose?"

He appeared at her side.

She took his arm and walked out.

The silence in the room was almost deafening as they all looked at one another.

"She really did it," Delia finally said. She'd opened her plastic heart. No gummy bears inside. No jelly beans. Just a small flash drive and a narrow slip of paper, folded in half.

"You going to see what it says?" Mac asked.

She shook her head and tossed the heart right back into the basket. "She knows we're all going to say yes no matter what's on the paper."

Everyone else's heart went back into the basket.

"Is this what her parties are always like?" Gage asked as he tossed his unopened heart in with the rest.

"She does like a little drama."

"A *little*?" Ali was breathing hard. "She's the

queen of it. So maybe I should tell you I think I'm in labor."

"Are you *sure*?"

"Whether she's sure or not…" Hayley was looking down at herself. "I am. My water just broke." She laughed breathlessly when Seth swept her off her feet and started from the room.

"She's *not* going to beat me." Ali was hunched over, cradling her belly with one hand and dragging Grant with her other.

"Who's got Noon-to-Midnight?"

"I was so sure it'd be the day after tomorrow!"

In a matter of minutes, the living room had vacated as the rush for the hospital was on.

Delia looked at Mac. "You know what this means."

He spread his hands a little. "Honey, you've had me in a tailspin from the first time I heard you laugh. You tell me what this means."

She pressed her lips to his. "I was right when I told you I wasn't an heiress. I'm not even going to win the baby pool. It's a good thing you've got the guesthouse locked down with Vivian. Who knows what she'll do next."

He laughed and dragged her down onto his knee. "As long as you marry me, Delia, I'm happy whatever you are."

They both heard the monumental sigh and looked over to see Montrose standing in the doorway with a serving tray in his hands. "*Another* wedding," he intoned as if he'd heard the worst news in the world. "I suppose you will be having it *here*."

"I suppose we will, Montrose," Delia said cheerfully.

"My life is truly complete," he deadpanned and turned to go. But his eyes met Delia's before he stepped ponderously from the room.

And he winked.

*   *   *   *   *

Don't miss
New York Times *bestselling author*
Allison Leigh's
next novel in
The Fortunes of Texas:
The Wedding Gift series.
Available May 2022
from Harlequin Special Edition.

#2893 ANYONE BUT A FORTUNE
The Fortunes of Texas: The Wedding Gift • by Judy Duarte

Self-made woman Sofia De Leon has heard enough about the old-money Fortune family to know that Beau Fortune is not to be trusted. And now that they are competing for the same business award, he is also her direct rival. It is just a hot Texas minute, though, before ambition begins warring with attraction...

#2894 FIRST COMES BABY...
Wild Rose Sisters • by Christine Rimmer

When Josie LeClaire went into labor alone on her farm, she had no one to turn to but her nearby fellow farmer, Miles Halstead. Fortunately, the widowed Miles was more than up to the task. But a marriage of convenience is only convenient until one side ends up with unrequited feelings. Will Miles be willing to let go of his fears, or will Josie be the one left out in the cold?

#2895 HOME IS WHERE THE HOUND IS
Furever Yours • by Melissa Senate

Animal rescue worker Bethany Robeson already has her hands full with an inherited house and an overweight pooch named Meatball. She doesn't dare make room for Shane Dupree, her former high school sweetheart, now a single dad. Bethany doesn't believe in starting over, but Shane, baby Wyatt and Meatball could be the family she always dreamed of...

#2896 THE WRANGLER RIDES AGAIN
Men of the West • by Stella Bagwell

For years, rugged cowboy Jim Carroway has been more at home with horses than with people. But when stunning nanny Tallulah O'Brien arrives to wrangle the kids of Three Rivers Ranch, she soon tempts him from the barn back to life. After Jim lost his pregnant wife, he thought he'd closed his heart forever. Can the vibrant, vivacious Tally convince him that it's never too late for love's second act?

#2897 THE HERO NEXT DOOR
Small-Town Sweethearts • by Carrie Nichols

Olive Downing has big dreams for her Victorian bed-and-breakfast. She doesn't need her handsome new neighbor pointing out the flaws in her plan. But Cal Pope isn't the average busybody. The gruff firefighter can be sweet, charming—and the perfect partner for the town fundraiser. Maybe there's a soft heart underneath his rough exterior that needs rescuing, too?

#2898 A MARRIAGE OF BENEFITS
Home to Oak Hollow • by Makenna Lee

Veterinarian Jessica Talbot wants to build a clinic and wildlife rescue. She could access her trust fund, but there's a caveat—Jessica needs a husband. When she learns Officer Jake Carter needs funding to buy and train his own K-9 partner, Jessica proposes. Jake is shocked, but he agrees—only for the money. It's the perfect plan—if only Jessica can avoid falling for her husband...and vice versa!

YOU CAN FIND MORE INFORMATION ON UPCOMING HARLEQUIN TITLES, FREE EXCERPTS AND MORE AT HARLEQUIN.COM.

HSECNM0122B

"I remember. I remember it all, Bethany."

Jeez. He hadn't meant for his voice to turn so serious,
so reverent. But there was very little chance of hiding his
real feelings when she was around.

"Me, too," she said.

For a few moments they ate in silence.

"Thanks for helping me here," she said. "You've done
a lot of that since I've been back."

"Anytime. And I mean that."

"Ditto," she said.

He reached over and squeezed her hand but didn't let
go. And suddenly he was looking—with that seriousness,
with that reverence—into those green eyes that had also

kept him up those nights when he couldn't stop thinking about her. They both leaned in at the same time, the kiss soft, tender, then with all the pent-up passion they'd clearly both been feeling these last days.

She pulled slightly away. "Uh-oh."

He let out a rough exhale, trying to pull himself together. "Right? You're leaving in a couple weeks. Maybe three tops. And I'm solely focused on being the best father I can be. So that's two really good reasons why we shouldn't kiss again." Except he leaned in again.

And so did she. This time there was nothing soft or tender about the kiss. Instead, it was pure passion. His hand wound in her silky brown hair, her hands on his face.

A puppy started barking, then another, then yet another. The three cockapoos.

"They're saving us from getting into trouble," Bethany said, glancing at the time on her phone. "Time for their potty break. They'll be interrupting us all night, so that should keep us in line."

He smiled. "We can get into a lot of trouble in between, though."

Don't miss
Home is Where the Hound Is *by Melissa Senate,*
available March 2022 wherever
Harlequin Special Edition books and ebooks are sold.

Harlequin.com

Get 4 FREE REWARDS!

We'll send you 2 FREE Books plus 2 FREE Mystery Gifts.

Harlequin Special Edition books relate to finding comfort and strength in the support of loved ones and enjoying the journey no matter what life throws your way.

FREE Value Over **$20**

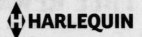
HARLEQUIN

Heartfelt or thrilling, passionate or uplifting—Harlequin is more than just happily-ever-after.

With twelve different series to choose from and new books available every month, you are sure to find stories that will move you, uplift you, inspire and delight you.

SIGN UP FOR THE HARLEQUIN NEWSLETTER

Be the first to hear about great new reads and exciting offers!

Harlequin.com/newsletters